For Beatrice
With love

Chapter 1

When she woke in the night, Sophie knew at once that something was wrong. There was a strange taste in her mouth, and an acrid smell filled her nostrils. At first, she thought it might be the smell of unfamiliarity. She wasn't sleeping in her own bed, in her own home, and the new smells of this room might be playing tricks on her. But she soon realised it was more than that. In her half-awake state, she instinctively knew that she shouldn't doze off again.

She coughed involuntarily and blinked her eyes open. As she did, the smell became more familiar. It was a burning smell. Smoke was coming from somewhere nearby. It was like the charred smell that comes into the house when a neighbour is burning leaves in their back garden or when one of the gas rings catches the handle of a saucepan.

She sat up, climbed out of bed, and opened her bedroom door. The smell wasn't as harsh out in the hallway, but she couldn't think where it might be coming from in her room. There was no sign of a fire, and when she turned the light on she couldn't see any smoke.

Walking over to the window, she drew back the curtains, and the sight that greeted her made her gasp in horror. The small museum that stood in the grounds of the house was on fire. Smoke and flames were pouring out of the front windows, and the treasures her elderly hosts Albert and Bunny had collected over their sixty years as archaeologists were in danger.

She grabbed her cardigan off a chair and bolted down the hallway to the main bedroom.

'Albert! Bunny!' she shouted, banging and clattering on the door. 'Wake up! The museum is on fire!'

When she didn't get an answer, she barged the door open and burst into the room in a panic. Bunny was fast asleep, and Albert was nowhere to be seen. She rushed over to the bed and shook Bunny awake.

'Bunny, the museum is on fire!' she yelled. 'Where's Albert?'

Bunny was still groggy from being woken up so abruptly.

'Albert?' she muttered. 'Didn't he come to bed then?'

On hearing this, Sophie was gripped with terror. She knew Albert liked to work late into the night and, when he did, he sometimes slept in a small room at the back of the museum. As Bunny struggled to wake up, Sophie rushed down the stairs, two steps at a time, and sprinted across the lawn towards the fire.

'Albert!' she shouted, her eyes watering from the smoke. 'Albert, are you in there?'

The heat was intolerable. It scorched her skin and singed her eyebrows and hair. Shards of glass were scattered across the lawn where the windows at the front had shattered, and thick black smoke billowed out through the gaps, pushing her back towards the house. It was impossible to get anywhere near the front of the museum. She would have to circle around to the other side and see if she could find a way in.

She rushed down the side of the building, coughing uncontrollably and blinking the smoky tears away from her eyes. The back of her throat felt cracked and dry. She was finding it hard to breathe. Pulling off her cardigan, she held it over her mouth and nose, but still the coughing continued.

At the back of the museum, the smoke was less

intense, but Sophie was shocked to find that the rear door was wide open. How had this happened? Albert was usually so diligent about security. Why would he leave a door open in the middle of the night? There was no time to worry about that now, though. She had to establish whether he was still inside and, if he was, find a way to get him out.

'Albert!' she shouted through the door. 'Albert, where are you?'

There was no response. An old rain barrel stood against the back wall just outside the door. She plunged her cardigan into it, then squeezed out the excess water and tied the sodden garment around her mouth and nose in an attempt to filter the smoke. Then, taking a deep breath, she stepped tentatively inside.

The front of the museum was now a roaring inferno. Sophie knew she didn't have much time. She got down onto her hands and knees to duck below the level of the smoke and squinted into the darkness of the interior. There was something stretched out on the floor a little further down. Within a few seconds, she could tell that it was Albert, and he didn't seem to be moving. With her eyes streaming from the effects of the smoke, she swallowed hard and started crawling down towards him.

When she finally reached Albert, he was barely conscious. Blood was seeping from a cut on the side of his head, forming a red pool on the hardwood floor. His eyes were only half open. He looked completely bewildered. Sophie reached out her hand and touched him lightly on the shoulder.

'Albert,' she said, her voice trembling with terror. 'Albert, are you alright?'

It took him a moment to recognise her. When he did, he grabbed hold of her arm and stared at her with desperation in his eyes.

'The relic,' he muttered. 'You must warn T.J.'

Sophie stared blankly back at him, wondering what this could mean.

'Come on,' she said. 'We've got to get you out of here.'

In the choking clouds of noxious smoke, Sophie knew they would have to be quick. Hoisting him up into a seated position, she held him under his arms and began to drag him back towards the open door. It was a tortuously slow process. Albert wasn't a big man, but the smoke was taking its toll, and Sophie's resolve and focus were fading fast.

A section of the ceiling crackled and collapsed at the front of the museum, sending flaming splinters and fragments powering through the air. Seconds later, Sophie realised her hair was on fire. She flapped at it in a panic, frantically trying to put it out, but no sooner had she stifled the flames than she noticed Albert's sleeve was alight. The smoke was now so thick she was finding it hard to breathe. She swayed on her feet for a moment, trying desperately not to pass out, but her strength was waning, and she was terrified that they were both about to perish.

As she hauled him out through the back door and dragged him onto the grass, the wailing sirens of the emergency services pierced the night air. Almost immediately, a member of the fire service was at the back of the building. He rushed over to where Sophie was still dragging Albert away from the burning museum.

'Two people at the back of the building, Sir!' he shouted into a two-way radio. 'One of them needs medical attention.'

He bent down to examine Albert, then picked him up and carried him away from the fire, laying him down on the grass some distance away. Dropping onto her knees, Sophie pulled the sodden cardigan off her face and inhaled the acrid air, coughing and spluttering in between gulps.

'Get an ambulance!' she shouted when she finally managed to stop coughing. 'Albert's badly injured. He must have fallen and banged his head on something.'

'It's on its way,' said the firefighter. 'What about you? Are you OK?'

Sophie didn't answer. She had descended into another coughing fit and was having trouble catching her breath.

A few minutes later, the ambulance arrived. It powered up to the front of the house, then rolled across the lawn to where Albert was lying. As the paramedics administered oxygen and examined the cut on his head, Bunny knelt by his side, trying to offer him some comfort. She was frantic with worry but desperate to hide her distress from Albert.

'How is he?' she asked. 'Is he going to be alright?'

'It's quite a nasty injury,' said the paramedic, 'so we'll need to get him to the hospital right away.'

Albert was still conscious, but he wasn't making much sense. He pushed the oxygen mask away from his face, grabbed hold of Bunny's arm, and pulled her in close.

'The Imperium,' he muttered. 'We have to stop them.'

Bunny swallowed hard. Her mouth was dry and tears were forming in her eyes. She held Albert's hand while they carried him to the ambulance, then she and Sophie followed in her car as the ambulance sped through the night with its flashing blue lights ablaze.

It was only when Albert was safely inside the hospital that Sophie allowed herself to think about what she had done. Despite being only twelve years old, she had rushed into a burning building and dragged a fully grown man out to safety. It was such a reckless thing to do. She could have been killed. The immensity of what she had done hit her like a bolt of lightning.

As the emotion welled up inside her, she started to shake and tears streamed down her face. Bunny seemed to understand. She held on to Sophie as it all came pouring out of her.

'That was a very foolish thing you did tonight,' said Bunny, the tears welling up in her own eyes. 'You could have died in there, and I would never have forgiven myself if anything had happened to you. But thank you. Thank you, you fabulous, brave girl. You saved my darling Albert, and I don't know how I can ever repay you.'

Chapter 2

The fierce wind battered against Sienna's face as she tumbled helplessly through space, thrown about like an autumn leaf caught up in a never-ending vortex. The noise was deafening. Bright lights exploded all around, making it hard for her to catch her breath. But she knew she had to hold her nerve. Not much further and she would arrive at her destination. Then the lights and noise rose to a violent crescendo and, as her feet crashed down onto something solid, she had to fight against the momentum to keep from tumbling to the ground.

For several seconds she stood perfectly still, trying to take in her surroundings. It was cold and dark, but the wet sand under her feet and the gentle sound of the waves hitting the shore helped to calm her fears. Everything was as it should be. She had landed on the beach in the dead of night when nobody was around to witness her arrival. It was the perfect time to travel through a portal from another world.

The jagged cliffs towered over her like a colossal wall of darkness, hiding her sudden appearance from the people of the town. In the distance, she could see the lights of Bramlington Bay flickering against a backdrop of houses and hotels. It was all so different from the home she had left behind on the parallel world of Galacdros. Her family and friends; the familiar sights and sounds. It would be quite a while before she could see them all again.

Something moved in the shadows, and Sienna's survival instincts immediately kicked into action. She dropped her backpack to the ground and spun around, ready to do battle.

'Who's there?' she shouted. 'Show yourself, now!'

Sienna was an accomplished martial artist and a genuine match for anyone in unarmed combat. She took a step forward, ready to take on whatever was lurking in the darkness.

A man loomed into view. Sienna couldn't tell whether he was armed.

'It's OK, Sienna,' he said. 'I'm not here to fight.'

'Who are you?' she barked. 'And how do you know my name?'

'My name is Fraser,' said the man. 'Jutan sent me to meet you. I'm one of her agents.'

Sienna studied him for a moment with her piercing, dark eyes. Like many people in her world, she was a highly skilled mind reader and telepath, and if he had any malicious intent, she was sure to pick it up. After a few seconds of scrutiny, she decided he wasn't an immediate threat. She lifted her backpack and slipped it onto her shoulder.

'I wasn't expecting anyone to be here,' she said, still a little on guard. 'How did you know where I would arrive?'

'Jutan always knows,' he said. 'She has an instinct for this sort of thing.'

On hearing his words, Sienna was now sure he was telling the truth. Jutan was a senior member of The Elite, a covert security force that operates on the margins of the two worlds. As Sienna's new commanding officer, she was the only person who knew she was on her way through the portal.

They set off down the beach towards the lights of the town. As they walked, Fraser briefed Sienna on her new role and told her she would meet with Jutan early the following morning.

'I've arranged an apartment for you on West Street,' he said. 'It's quite near the station, and most of the shops you'll need are close by.'

'Yes, I know West Street,' Sienna replied. 'I lived in this town for three months in the summer of last year.'

'So I heard,' said Fraser. 'Your victory over Osorio was a great day for Galacdros. It's good to have you here on our team.'

Eight months earlier Sienna had travelled to this world on her first mission for The Elite. At sixteen years of age, she was the youngest agent on the force, and she was on the trail of Osorio, a dangerous fugitive who had stolen a precious artefact called The Orb of Nendaro. Her mission was to recover The Orb and return it to its rightful place in the Galacdros Senate.

It was an arduous mission, and at times her life had been in great danger. But despite facing several setbacks, her relentless drive and indomitable spirit never waned. Eventually, she cornered Osorio on a houseboat in central London and, after a titanic struggle, she finally recovered the prize she had been searching for.

When she returned triumphantly to Galacdros, she was feted as a conquering hero. It was a glorious day, but Sienna knew she would never have completed her mission had it not been for the help of Sophie Watson, a friend she made on first arriving in this world. Now she was back in Bramlington Bay, she was keen to see her good friend again.

When they reached the beach café, they climbed up the steps onto the promenade and headed into the heart of the town. Everything seemed very familiar to Sienna. It was as if she had only been away for a day or two.

The apartment was in a small block on the corner of West Street. It had a large window in the living area that gave her a good view of the surrounding streets, and from the bedroom, she could see right down to the beach. Fraser gave her a brief tour, then handed her a small bunch of keys.

'Jutan would like to meet you on the seafront tomorrow morning at seven-thirty,' he said. 'There's a bench on the promenade, just down from the tourist office. Wait there for her, and she will find you.' Then he wished her good luck and left.

It was a great relief to Sienna to have the apartment to herself. The journey through the portal from Galacdros had lasted less than sixty seconds, but the impact of travelling in such a way had taken its toll on her strength. Within minutes of Fraser leaving, she was sound asleep on the bed.

She was awoken the following morning by the screeching cry of the seagulls. After a good night's rest, she felt rejuvenated and refreshed, and she was keen to get up and out to meet her new commanding officer. The sun was already up, but the town was still asleep.

Rifling through the well-stocked kitchen, she picked over the selection of foods that Fraser had left for her. She was a stranger in a strange land and many of them were unfamiliar and odd. Eventually, she found some bread that she recognised from her last visit to this world. She toasted up a few slices, ate them with butter and jam, then filled up her water bottle and set off through the quiet streets towards the seafront.

It was a crisp, clear morning, and the town was just waking up. As she walked along the promenade, a gentle breeze was coming in off the sea, and hungry seagulls circled noisily above the deserted beach. Occasionally one of them would swoop to the ground, looking for a tiny morsel that might provide them with a decent breakfast. They watched Sienna suspiciously as they pecked at what they had found, their beady eyes keeping her under constant surveillance.

In the distance, Sienna could see Kestrel Island,

sitting serenely on the horizon. It looked so peaceful on this clear spring morning, in stark contrast to the terror she and Sophie had faced the previous summer. Under the cover of darkness, they had travelled out to the island on the trail of Osorio. But when they were discovered by armed guards they had to run for their lives, and suddenly they had become the prey. It was a harrowing experience. For several hours they were shot at and hunted down like wild animals. Had it not been for Sophie's grit and determination, they may never have made it off the island alive.

On reaching the meeting point, Sienna dropped her backpack onto the promenade bench and checked the time on her watch. It was seven twenty-four. She was early. But there was no time to sit and enjoy the scenery. Glancing to her left, she saw a tall, elegantly dressed woman striding purposefully in her direction. Jutan may have been past the official retirement age, but she had the gait and athleticism of someone thirty years younger and an air of confidence that inspired everyone who worked for her. As she approached the bench, Sienna turned to greet her.

'Good morning, Sienna,' said Jutan, smiling warmly. 'It's good to see you looking so refreshed. I trust you slept well.'

'Very well, thank you,' Sienna answered. 'And thank you for inviting me to be a member of your team. I'm looking forward to getting started.'

They sat down on the promenade bench. There was nobody else around.

'The work you have already carried out for The Elite has been very impressive,' said Jutan, 'and I'm pleased that you accepted the position.'

She reached inside her coat pocket and took out a phone and a folded sheet of paper.

'As you're already familiar with this world, I'd like you to start work straight away. I've put the details of your mission onto this phone. You can allow yourself one hour to study the files, then you should delete them for security reasons.'

She handed the phone to Sienna. It looked very familiar. It was the same model she had used when she was last working in this world.

'If you look in the file called Operation,' Jutan continued, 'you'll see some photos of the man I'd like you to locate. His name is Silver, and it's urgent we find out where he is.'

Sienna opened up the file and scrolled through a series of photographs. They were all of a well-built man with a penetrating stare and a small scar on the side of his head. He was elegantly dressed, and he displayed a confidence that bordered on arrogance.

'Silver?' said Sienna, staring at the photographs intently. 'Where have I heard that name before?'

'Last week he escaped from The Stockade, the maximum-security prison on Galacdros. He is a very dangerous man and our contacts believe he is now hiding out in this world.'

'But why would he want to come here?'

'He is searching for a sacred Mayan artefact,' said Jutan. 'While he was in prison, he talked constantly to the other prisoners about an ancient relic that he believes contains great power. It is thought to be here in England, and Silver thinks that possessing it could make him invincible.'

She handed Sienna the folded sheet of paper. It contained a detailed sketch of an irregularly shaped object with a series of engravings of trees on it.

'Very few people have ever seen this relic, so we only have an artist's impression of what it might look like. It was found in a secret Mayan tomb in Guatemala in the early 1960s, but it disappeared shortly after the tomb was opened. It is said to hold the key to immortality.'

'Immortality?' said Sienna. 'It didn't do much good for whoever they buried in that tomb, did it?'

'And it may not be helping whoever still possesses it either,' said Jutan. 'Herbert Hawkins was the leader of that expedition and, when he died, he left his entire collection to his only son Rufus. Three days ago the police found Rufus dead at his home in the Yorkshire Dales. The house had been completely ransacked, and the case is being treated as murder.'

'And you think Silver might be responsible?'

'I'm afraid so. And if he didn't find what he was looking for, he may not have stopped there. There were two young archaeologists working with Hawkins on that dig. We're still trying to establish who they were, but last night another well-known expert on Mayan culture was mysteriously injured at his home not far from here. Albert Robson had an extensive collection of Mayan artefacts in a museum he built in the grounds of his country home, Abbeville House. He is now recuperating in hospital and the museum has been destroyed in a fire.'

'Has he been able to tell the police what happened?' Sienna asked.

'Unfortunately, they haven't been able to interview him yet,' said Jutan. 'He took a heavy blow to the head, so he's still under sedation in the hospital. And sadly Rufus Hawkins is in no position to tell us anything.'

Jutan paused for a moment, looking for the right words to say.

'There's something else you should know,' she said. 'Silver believes he's an innocent man who was unjustly sent to The Stockade because the authorities in Galacdros were intimidated by his power and influence. He has vowed to take revenge on the committee of senators who imprisoned him, and that committee was led by your father, Memphis.'

Sienna was alarmed to hear that her father's life was in danger. She had always been inspired by his impeccable record as a highly decorated officer in The Elite, but Memphis wasn't the fighter he had been when he was younger. The years he had spent working as a Galacdros senator had slowed him down considerably. It was vital she located this fugitive before he could harm her father.

'So what do we know about Silver?' she asked.

'Well, we know he's not a telepath, but he is highly intelligent and fiercely ambitious. And he's prepared to destroy anyone who gets in his way.'

Sienna studied the photographs again. There was a

disturbing coldness about Silver's demeanour. She found it a little unnerving.

'You said he believes that he's an innocent man,' she said. 'What was he sent to prison for?'

'Countless acts of violence and corruption that were driven by his lust for power,' said Jutan. 'It's all there in the files. He has such a sense of entitlement that he believes the law doesn't apply to him. But eventually, his arrogance got the better of him and he started to make mistakes.'

'So where do you think I should start looking for him?' Sienna asked.

'Perhaps the best place to start would be that museum at Abbeville House. Ask a few questions. See if anyone knows how the fire started. You could pose as a tourist in the area. After all, it's not that far from the truth.'

'OK,' said Sienna. 'And where exactly is this Abbeville House?'

'It's about thirty miles north-east of here. Can you drive a car?'

'Well, I've never tried, but it doesn't look all that hard.'

'In that case, we may need to have a rethink.'

'I can ride a motorcycle,' said Sienna. 'When I was

living here last summer, John Hodgson, the owner of The Grand Hotel, taught me to ride the little motorbike he used for buzzing around the town.'

'Splendid,' said Jutan. 'I'll ask Fraser to get you one of those straight away. Perhaps you could pop out to Abbeville House later today and take a look around. And keep Fraser up to date with anything that you find out. His number is on your phone. It's listed as F.E. Electrical.'

Jutan stood up and prepared to leave, then turned to have a final word with Sienna.

'You were bold and courageous on your last mission,' she said, 'but I would advise you to approach this case with a lot more caution. Silver is a ruthless man who has a disturbing view of the world. He values nobody's life except his own, and now he is being driven by a lust for revenge, he will be an even bigger threat. If you get a sighting of him, call for reinforcements. We don't want any dead heroes on our hands.'

Chapter 3

By the time Sophie and Bunny returned to Abbeville
House, the sun was already creeping above the horizon.
The doctors had fully examined Albert, and he was now
sleeping comfortably at the hospital. He hadn't been
able to give any details about what had happened at the
museum. The blow he took to his head had left him
quite confused.

Throughout the journey home, Bunny kept trying to
put on a brave face, talking about how good the doctors
had been and how Albert couldn't be in safer hands. But
underneath it all, Sophie could tell that something had
unnerved her; something that she wasn't telling Sophie
the full story about.

Once they were safely inside the house, the fatigue
seemed to take its toll on Bunny. Sophie thought she
looked a little smaller than usual, and her energy

appeared to have drained away.

'You must be exhausted,' said Sophie. 'Why don't you have a nap? Then we can have a bit of a tidy up after breakfast.'

'Yes, I think I will,' said Bunny, smiling back at her and giving her a hug. 'You know, I don't know how I'd have dealt with this if I'd been on my own. It's a real comfort to have you here with me.'

'I'm very glad that I'm here, too,' Sophie answered, keen to offer her some reassurance. She took Bunny by the arm and walked with her up the stairs to her bedroom.

'Don't let me sleep too long,' said Bunny. 'I'm supposed to phone the hospital at eleven o'clock.'

'OK,' said Sophie. 'If I don't hear you moving around by ten forty-five, I'll bring you up a cup of tea.'

While Bunny slept, Sophie went out to the garden and tried to come to terms with the horror of the previous night. It was a stroke of good fortune that she had woken up and discovered the fire, and even luckier that she and Albert managed to get out of the museum alive. But how had this happened? Albert was normally so careful.

Staring into the charred ruins of the museum, she thought about the small gold relic that Albert had given her the previous afternoon. It was a curious-looking object and, thinking back, she remembered how strange their meeting had been.

It had been late in the day when he called her into his office at the back of the museum. On the table there was a small metal box, which he opened reverentially. Inside was a silk cloth, and wrapped within it was a little twist of gold.

'I don't think I've ever shown you this before,' he said, picking up the relic. 'I came across it when we excavated a Mayan tomb in the summer of 1961.'

He held it out to her in the palm of his hand. It was an odd shape. It looked like a piece of a puzzle.

'The native guide who worked with us claimed it had extraordinary powers,' he continued, 'but for almost sixty years it has been sitting here in this metal box.'

He paused for a moment as if he was unsure how to proceed. Finally, he appeared to make up his mind.

'I'd like you to have it,' he said, more forcefully than seemed natural.

'Oh Albert, I couldn't,' said Sophie. 'It's part of your collection.'

'No, please take it,' he answered. 'It doesn't really belong here, anyway.'

Sophie wasn't sure what to do. She was a guest at his house, so it would have been rude to turn him down, but she didn't know what she would do with this strange-looking object.

'OK,' she said, finally. 'Thank you, Albert. That's very kind of you.'

'But you must promise me you will keep it safe,' he said, with a hint of urgency in his voice. 'And keep it out of sight. We wouldn't want it to fall into the wrong hands.'

'What wrong hands?' Sophie asked. 'Is it valuable then?'

'All these works are valuable in their own way,' said Albert. 'It just depends on who is making the judgment.'

He wrapped the relic in the silk cloth, carefully put it back in the small metal box, and handed it over to her. Sophie thought he seemed unusually on edge. It was difficult to know what to make of it.

Now, thinking about the relic the following day, she wondered if it might be connected to the fire. When she found Albert on the floor of the museum, he mentioned the relic and told her she must warn T.J. But who was T.J.? And what was Albert talking about when he told Bunny 'We have to stop them'? Whatever was going on, it was completely out of character, and Sophie was determined to get to the bottom of it.

When Bunny called the hospital later that morning, the news was a little better. The doctor told her Albert was awake and in good spirits but, as he had suffered a head injury, they were keeping him in for a couple of days just to keep an eye on him. Bunny was massively relieved, and it seemed to lift her spirits.

Just before lunch, there was a knock at the front door. When Sophie peered out through the window, she could see a police car parked outside and two men were standing on the doorstep. One of them was wearing a police uniform, and the other was wearing a dark grey suit. She opened the door just as they were about to knock again.

'Good morning,' said the man in the suit. 'I'm Detective Sergeant Davis and this is Constable Perkins. Would it be possible to speak to Mrs Robson about last night's fire?'

'Of course,' said Sophie. 'Would you like to come in?'

She stepped aside to let them into the hall, then showed them into the sitting room where Bunny was nursing a hot cup of tea.

'Bunny, these police officers would like to talk to you about the fire,' said Sophie. Then she turned to the men and offered them a cup of tea.

'Thank you, but we've just had lunch,' said the detective, before the other officer could reply. Sophie could tell that Constable Perkins wasn't very happy about it.

'What about you, Constable?' she asked. 'Can I tempt you?'

The constable shifted awkwardly on his feet. 'Well, I erm—'

'Go on, Perkins,' said the detective. 'Have a drink if you want one.'

'Oh, right,' said Perkins, a little nervously. Then he turned and smiled at Sophie. 'Thank you. Milk and no sugar would be lovely.'

Sophie went out to the kitchen and quickly rustled up a cup of tea for him. When she returned, the men were sitting opposite Bunny, and Constable Perkins was studiously writing on a small notepad. She put the tea on the table next to him.

'Oh, thank you very much,' he said. 'That's very kind.'

Sophie smiled back at him and took a seat next to Bunny.

'And I believe you're currently staying here as a guest of Mrs Robson,' said the detective, turning his gaze towards Sophie.

'Erm, yes,' said Sophie. 'My mum and dad are in Paris celebrating their wedding anniversary, and Bunny and Albert kindly invited me to stay with them.'

'We've known Sophie since she was a baby,' said Bunny. 'It's always a pleasure to have her staying here.'

'And am I right in thinking that you were the first person to reach the fire?' the detective asked.

'Yes, that's right,' Sophie answered. 'I woke up in the night and thought I could smell smoke. When I discovered the museum was on fire, I ran down to wake Bunny and Albert. But Albert wasn't in his bed, so I rushed out to see if I could find him.'

'And could you tell us what you found?'

'Well,' said Sophie. 'I couldn't get near the front of the museum. It was too hot, and smoke was pouring out of the windows. So I ran around to the back to see if there was another way in. Fortunately, the back door was open, and I was able to get inside and drag Albert out.'

'The back door was open?' said the detective, sounding a little surprised. 'Was it normal for Mr Robson to leave the door of the museum open at night?'

'Oh no,' said Bunny. 'Albert is very diligent about security, and we have a very sophisticated burglar alarm fitted.'

'Then why would the back door be open?' the detective asked.

'I don't know,' Sophie answered. 'But I was very glad that it was.'

The detective paused for a few seconds, eyeing Sophie curiously.

'Do you mind if I ask how old you are?' he said, eventually.

'I'm twelve,' Sophie answered. 'I'll be thirteen in June.'

'Dragging a grown man out of a burning building was an extraordinary act of bravery for a twelve-year-old,' said the detective, 'particularly for a girl.'

'What do you mean, particularly for a girl?' Bunny barked at him indignantly. 'Why should her being a girl make any difference? Amelia Earhart was a girl; Rosa Parks was a girl. Women are just as capable of showing courage as men, detective.'

'Well, yes, of course,' said the detective, looking totally chastened. 'I... I didn't mean any offence. I just meant that—'

'I think we all know what you meant, detective,' Bunny retorted, putting him in his place. 'But I won't have any of that kind of talk in my house.'

Sophie caught sight of the constable sipping on his tea. He was holding the cup close to his face to hide the smile that he was finding it difficult to stifle.

'Erm, could we take a look at the museum?' said the detective, looking to change the subject.

They left the house and walked across the garden to the burnt-out museum. The front of the building was badly damaged, but most of the structure was still reasonably intact. Through a gap where the window had once been, Sophie could see the fire investigators sifting through the debris. Only a few hours earlier this building had been a roaring inferno; a potential death trap for anyone who had been inside.

'Have you been able to establish whether anything can be salvaged?' the detective asked.

'No, I haven't,' Bunny answered. 'The Fire Service asked me to stay off the site until they have concluded their investigation.'

Sophie found it heartbreaking to see how many precious works had been destroyed. Some of the displays at the front of the museum were so badly burnt that they were unrecognizable. As she gazed at the scorched remains of the exhibits, the memory of her desperate struggle to drag Albert out through the back door suddenly flashed into her mind. It sent her into a cold sweat.

'Sixty years it took us to collect all those exhibits,' said Bunny, shaking her head with sadness. 'A lot of them are irreplaceable. How could something like this happen?'

'Did your husband have any enemies that you know of?' the detective asked, peering through the blackened window frame.

'Not that I can think of,' Bunny replied.

'Albert's a very popular figure locally,' said Sophie. 'Everybody loves him. What made you ask that?'

'Well, the Chief Fire Officer thinks this may not have been an accident. He thinks the fire could have been started deliberately. And according to the doctors, the blow that Mr Robson took to his head wasn't an accident either.'

'Are you trying to tell us that someone attacked Albert, then set the museum alight?' said Bunny, barely able to believe what she was hearing. 'But why on earth would someone do that?'

'That's what we have to find out,' said the detective.

Sophie was now even more convinced that the small

gold relic was connected to the fire. She considered telling the police about it, but something stopped her from doing so. Albert had entrusted the relic to her and told her she must keep it out of sight, and she was determined to stop it from falling into the wrong hands.

If only she could talk to her friend Sienna. They had been through so much in the short time they had known each other. She was sure Sienna would know exactly what to do. But the girls hadn't seen one another for over three months, and she didn't know if Sienna would ever be coming back. It looked like Sophie would have to deal with this on her own.

After lunch, Bunny fell asleep in an armchair with her cat Banjo sprawled out by her feet, so Sophie decided to go back up to her room. Opening up her backpack, she took out the small metal box and examined the gold relic that Albert had given her the previous afternoon. What was so valuable about this little twist of gold? How could something so innocuous justify leaving a man barely conscious on the floor of a burning building? And why had Albert given the relic to her? Did he know someone was looking for it? Whatever his motive was, Sophie knew that whoever attacked Albert was still out there, and they might decide to come back to search Abbeville House.

Out of the corner of her eye, she noticed some movement at the far end of the driveway. Someone on a motorcycle had paused at the gates and appeared to be sizing up the house. Sophie moved across to the window and watched them from behind the curtain. The rider waited for a few seconds, then turned the bike into the driveway and began moving slowly up the gravel towards her.

As the motorcycle approached, Sophie watched it nervously. The helmet and dark visor obscured the rider's face, making them look like an android. It stopped in front of the burnt-out museum. The rider peered into the ruins for a minute before turning the bike and bringing it around towards the front of the house.

Could this be the person who was responsible for Albert's injuries? Sophie stashed the relic back in the secret hiding place at the bottom of her backpack and peered out from behind the curtain to see what the rider would do next. The bike came to a halt just below her window. A few anxious seconds passed as the rider stared up at the house, appearing to study it in great detail.

For a moment, Sienna sat and gazed at the majestic beauty of Abbeville House. Then she turned off the ignition, hoisted the bike up onto its stand, and breathed a sigh of relief. It had been a long ride from Bramlington Bay, and this was the first time she had ridden a motorcycle for several months. But she knew this was not the time to relax. She took a few long, slow breaths, reminding herself that it was important to stay alert. Despite the idyllic setting, the person responsible for the fire in the museum could still be around. Perhaps it was someone who was staying at the house. And perhaps that person was Silver.

Taking another deep breath, she lifted her helmet off, shook out her dark hair and stared up at the window where she had just seen the curtain move. Someone was watching her. She had better be on her guard.

Chapter 4

The shock of discovering the mysterious rider was actually Sienna made Sophie completely lose control. She shrieked with joy, stormed out of her bedroom door, and bounded down the stairs in a frenzy of excitement.

Sienna was still in defensive mode, cautiously eyeing up the house. When she saw the door starting to open, she leapt from the bike and stood ready to defend herself. But nothing could have prepared her for what came next. Sophie burst through the door onto the gravel path and ran towards her, screaming with delight.

'Sienna!' she shouted, flinging her arms around her and almost knocking her forcefully to the ground.

For a few seconds, they were both too excited to talk. Then Sophie couldn't contain herself any longer.

'How long have you been back? How did you know where to find me? Where did you get that motorcycle?'

The questions came pouring out of her in a frantic wave of euphoria.

'I arrived last night,' said Sienna. 'And I can't believe I've run into you so soon. What are you doing here?'

'This is Abbeville House,' said Sophie. 'It belongs to my friends Bunny and Albert. I'm staying here while my mum and dad are in Paris, celebrating their wedding anniversary.'

'It's gorgeous,' said Sienna. 'It's like a country mansion.'

Sophie didn't respond. She was so brimming over with excitement; she didn't know what to say first.

'I was sorry to hear about the fire at the museum,' said Sienna. 'I hope you weren't in any danger.'

'Well, she wouldn't have been,' said a voice from behind them, 'if she hadn't rushed into the burning building and rescued my darling husband Albert.'

Sophie spun around to see Bunny standing on the doorstep. She knew she would have to do some quick thinking to explain Sienna's sudden arrival.

'Oh, Bunny, this is my friend Sienna,' she said. 'I texted her this morning to tell her about the fire, and she called over to see if she could help.'

'Hello, Sienna,' said Bunny. 'It's very nice to meet you. Are you the young lady who was working for

Sophie's mother last year when she first became a Member of Parliament?'

'Yes, that's right,' said Sienna. 'Mrs Watson was kind enough to let me stay at her house, so I wanted to help out as much as I could.'

'Yes, Michelle speaks very highly of you, Sienna. Please come inside. I was about to put the kettle on.'

The girls settled themselves into the sitting room while Bunny went out to the kitchen to make a pot of tea. Sophie was still buzzing with excitement. She couldn't stop smiling, and she looked as if she might explode with happiness.

'It's so good to see you again,' she said. 'I can't believe you just turned up here out of the blue.'

Sienna was feeling equally euphoric. 'Well, to be honest, when I came up the driveway you were the last person I expected to bump into.'

They began to laugh, then leant forward and gave each other a hug.

'So what are you doing here?' Sophie asked, still smiling broadly.

Sienna looked towards the door to check that Bunny wasn't close by.

'Jutan asked me to come here to take a look at the

museum,' she said in a low voice. 'We're trying to track down a man called Silver. He escaped from a Galacdros prison last week, and we think he might have something to do with last night's fire.'

'With the fire?' said Sophie. 'But what would someone from Galacdros want from the Abbeville House museum?'

'He's looking for a sacred relic that was found in a Mayan tomb, and the museum had a lot of Mayan artefacts on display.'

At the mention of a Mayan tomb, Sophie felt a little alarmed. She thought about the relic Albert had given her the previous afternoon and wondered whether it could be what Silver was after.

'What did this relic look like?' she asked.

Sienna felt around in her pocket and took out the folded sheet of paper containing the artist's impression of the relic. It was a rough sketch, and even though it didn't look like the little twist of gold Albert had given Sophie, there were a few similarities.

'Albert gave me something like this yesterday afternoon, and I think it could be connected to the fire,' said Sophie.

'What did he say about it? Did he say where he got it from?'

'Yes. He said it was a sacred relic from a Mayan tomb, and that he didn't want it to fall into the wrong hands.'

She paused for a moment when she saw Sienna's eyes widen.

'Do you think this is what the fire was all about?' she asked.

'It's possible,' said Sienna.

'Then why did Albert give it to me?'

'That relic has been nothing but trouble since the day Albert got his hands on it,' said Bunny, carrying a tray of teacups into the room. 'I'm sorry, Sophie. I couldn't help overhearing what you were saying, and I'm horrified to discover that you have that dreadful thing.'

'Albert gave it to me a few hours before the fire,' said Sophie. 'He asked me to keep it safe. Do you think he knew he was about to get an unwelcome visitor?'

'We've been expecting an unwelcome visitor for almost sixty years,' Bunny replied. 'That relic has bad energy connected to it. I wouldn't even let Albert keep it in the house.'

She put the tray down on a small table and handed them a cup of tea each. There was also a plate of biscuits, which she offered to the girls before sitting down in the armchair next to Sophie.

'I'm sorry to hear about your husband, Bunny,' said Sienna. 'I hope he's going to be OK.'

'Thank you,' said Bunny. 'I'm sure he'll be fine. The doctor said he just needs to rest for a few days. He may be eighty-three now, but he still has the heart of a lion.'

'The police think someone might have attacked him, and then set fire to the museum,' said Sophie. 'So maybe they were after the relic.'

'Did they come to the house?' Sienna asked.

'No,' said Sophie. 'By the time we discovered the museum was on fire, they were long gone.'

'So they left empty-handed and didn't search the house? That's a bit odd.'

'Yes, it is strange,' said Bunny. 'It was the obvious place to look next.'

Thinking back to the previous night, Sophie realised how fortunate she and Bunny had been. They would both have been asleep if anyone had broken into the house, and they could easily have suffered the same fate as Albert. It was such a lucky escape.

'How did Albert get hold of the relic in the first place?' said Sienna, looking across at Bunny. 'Was he the person who opened the tomb?'

'No, he wasn't,' said Bunny. 'Herbert Hawkins was

the senior archaeologist on that dig, so he would have been the first one into the tomb. Albert was just starting out on his career. He was young and enthusiastic, and he signed up to work as one of Hawkins' assistants. He shared his duties with another young archaeologist called T.J. Stapleton.'

'T.J. Stapleton?' Sophie gasped. 'So that's what Albert was talking about when I found him on the floor of the museum. He told me I must warn T.J.'

'Lovely Albert,' said Bunny, 'always looking out for other people.'

'So if Hawkins was the leader, how did Albert end up taking the relic?' Sienna asked.

'He didn't,' said Bunny. 'None of them did, really. When they opened the tomb, they found three almost identical relics displayed on a ceremonial altar. Each of them had been individually made so they would fit together in a sort of puzzle. They were there so the occupant of the tomb could unite them once they had reached the next world. Then they would be at one with the gods.'

'Did Hawkins ever try to unite the relics himself?' Sienna asked. 'Having found the tomb, he must have been curious to see the finished puzzle.'

'No, he was never tempted. The native guide warned Hawkins that he should not attempt to complete the puzzle. He said the relics contained great power, but trying to exploit that power for personal gain could incur the wrath of the gods and his life would be cursed. So as there were three pieces, Hawkins decided the archaeologists should take one relic each.'

On hearing Bunny's story, Sophie knew immediately why the relic she had didn't match Sienna's rough sketch. It was only part of the puzzle. Albert had only given her one of the three pieces.

'From that moment on, Hawkins always referred to the combined relics as the Imperium,' said Bunny. 'It loosely translates as "the power". And the three of them agreed they would never discuss their secret with the outside world.'

'You said the native guide told Hawkins the relics contained great power,' said Sienna. 'What sort of power did he mean?'

'I don't know. There was an inscription on a stone tablet at the side of the altar that the guide deciphered for them. It read, "When these three worlds are united; the power of the gods will run through them".'

'And now someone is trying to find the relics so they

can gain access to that power,' said Sophie. 'That's not good news for Mr Hawkins or T.J. Stapleton.'

'It's not good news for you either,' said Sienna. 'If they didn't find what they wanted last night, they might come back to have another look. And this time they'll probably search the house.'

'We have to warn the others,' said Sophie. 'Their lives might be in danger.'

'I'm afraid it's too late for Herbert Hawkins,' said Bunny. 'He died a long time ago.'

'What about T.J. Stapleton?' Sophie asked.

'Nobody has heard from Stapleton for quite some time.'

'We have to find him,' said Sophie. 'Albert wanted me to warn him.'

Bunny didn't respond. She stood up and walked across to the window, a troubled look on her face. Sophie could tell that her mind was in turmoil. She had never seen her look so ill at ease. Staring at the burnt-out shell of the museum, Bunny shook her head, then turned back to face the girls.

'I can't let you get involved in this, Sophie,' she said. 'I promised your mother I would keep you safe, and I intend to keep my word. Whoever attacked Albert last night, and did this to our lovely museum, may be desperate to get their hands on the Imperium. I could never forgive myself if anything happened to you.'

'But couldn't we find out where Mr Stapleton is and phone him up? There can't be anything risky in that.'

Bunny turned and stared silently out of the window. She looked fearful and unsettled. The events of the last twenty-four hours had clearly shaken her.

A car appeared at the far end of the driveway. It was a large black car with tinted windows. It cruised through the gates and powered up the gravel, parking a few feet away from the museum.

'Oh no, what now?' said Bunny, sounding as if this was the last thing she needed.

Sophie and Sienna exchanged a glance, then stood up and walked across to join her by the window. They watched the car as three men climbed out. Sienna recognised one of the men immediately. It was Silver. As she had feared, he was back to take another look for the relic.

He was a big man, and even from some distance away, Sophie could tell that the other two men were intimidated by him. They seemed to cower in his presence. It wasn't just his size. It was his whole bearing and demeanour. Despite his elegant appearance, he had a cold and callous manner, as if nothing could arouse his sympathy. He looked like someone who was comfortable with cruelty.

He walked over to the burnt-out museum and pushed the front door over with the sole of his boot. Then he turned around, lifted his head and stared menacingly towards the house. His icy gaze chilled Sophie to the bone. She instinctively knew that something was wrong.

'Bunny, are all the doors and windows locked?' said Sienna, a note of urgency in her voice.

'Yes, I think so. Why, what's the matter?'

'I think those could be the men who were here last night. And it doesn't look like this is a social call.'

Chapter 5

Sienna grabbed Sophie and Bunny by the arm and pulled them away from the window.

'Don't let them see us,' she said. 'We can't allow them to know there's anyone at home.'

She knew they only had a few seconds before Silver would be at the front door. If he found them in the house, their lives would be in mortal danger.

For a moment, she thought about bolting out through the back door and hiding somewhere in the gardens. But Bunny would never be able to outrun these men. Their best chance was to stay inside the house and hope they could find somewhere to hide.

'Upstairs! Quickly!' she said, dragging them across the room and into the hallway.

It was a good thing they had seen the car arrive. By the time they reached the top of the stairs, the men were knocking aggressively on the front door.

'If we keep quiet, maybe they'll give up and go away,' said Bunny.

But the men had no intention of leaving. Within seconds, one of them smashed something solid into the door. On the third strike, it flew open and crashed against the inside wall, shattering the ornate glass in the door into tiny fragments. The violence of the men's entry shocked Bunny into action.

'Quickly, this way,' she whispered, leading them down the landing towards a room at the back of the house.

It was quite a basic bedroom with a large bed, a chest of drawers, and an ornate fireplace over against one wall. Sienna couldn't see any obvious escape route, and there was nowhere for them to hide. So why had Bunny dragged them into such a dead end? The three of them now looked like they were trapped.

But when Bunny pressed a tiny button on the underside of the mantelpiece and started pulling it towards her, Sienna could see at once that the fireplace wasn't real. It was actually a door with a secret space behind that was big enough for all three of them to hide. She stepped forward and helped Bunny to pull the fireplace door open. Then once the three of them were safely inside, she grabbed the interior handle and pulled the door shut again.

'Albert put this here a long time ago to hide some of our collection,' Bunny whispered, still trying to catch her breath. 'But since we've had the museum, it hasn't been used at all.'

It was pitch black inside the tiny space, and there was barely enough room for them all to squeeze in. As soon as Sienna pulled the door shut, Sophie could feel the claustrophobia building up inside her. She tried to slow her breathing down to control the rising panic, but it was a massive internal struggle.

'Are you OK?' Sienna whispered, aware that her friend was experiencing a crisis.

'I'm not sure how long I can do this,' Sophie answered, gripping Sienna's hand and taking a deep breath.

They could hear the men downstairs tearing through the house and, above the noise, Silver's voice barking out orders. Bunny was repulsed by the thought of these brutish men going through her possessions. They were her personal treasures, lovingly collected over a lifetime, and it was heartbreaking to hear them being treated so roughly. At one point, it sounded as if they had tipped her beloved cabinet over onto the floor. It was followed by the sound of crashing and smashing glass and more aggressive shouting from Silver.

It was difficult for Bunny to hold back the tears, but Sienna knew that there was nothing any of them could do. These men had already attacked Albert and left him for dead in a burning building. If they tried to intervene, they were likely to meet the same fate. There was no other option but to sit tight and hope that they weren't discovered.

After another resounding crash, they heard footsteps on the stairs. The men were getting closer. Sophie clenched her jaw and tried to keep her breathing slow and steady. The adrenaline was pumping through her, and her neck and shoulders were rigid and tense. She took another deep breath and tried to stop it from escalating into all-out panic.

'Where's the relic?' Sienna whispered.

'It's in my room,' said Sophie. 'But it's in a secret compartment in my backpack, so there's a chance they might not find it.'

The men searched through the bedrooms, ransacking wardrobes and drawers and tipping the contents out onto the floor. It wasn't long before they were in the room next door, and Sophie knew they were rifling through her belongings. They seemed to be in there for ages. She thought about the photograph of her mum and dad on the bedside table and wished there had been time to take it with her. It was nauseating to think that any of those men might touch it.

Eventually, the men's voices became louder and, with Silver shouting aggressively, they entered the room where Bunny and the girls were hiding. Sophie could feel the walls closing in, and her breathing became ragged and jerky. These were the men who had treated Albert so brutally, and now they were only a few feet away from where she was hiding. She closed her eyes and tried to think about wide-open spaces. It wasn't easy with Silver's malevolent presence on the other side of the wall.

'It's in this house somewhere,' Silver barked, 'and I'm not leaving until we've found it. Have a look up that chimney. He may have stashed it up there.'

One of the men began to investigate the fireplace. He was only a few inches away from them. They could hear him grunting and breathing as he poked and prodded around. Sienna pulled hard on the handle on the inside of the door, trying to ensure that the fireplace stayed flush against the wall.

'It's not a real fireplace,' the man said. 'It's only here to tart the room up a bit.'

On hearing his words, Sophie nearly passed out with fear. Their secret was out. Surely it was now just a matter of time before they were discovered. She stared into the darkness that surrounded her, petrified that Silver was about to find them.

Seconds later, they heard Silver's voice on the other side of the fireplace. Even with a wall between them, Sophie could sense his murderous intent. He ran his hands over every surface, manically looking for a breakthrough; anything that would help him find the relic. It was a terrifying experience. He had an animal-like presence, like a big cat that was stalking its prey. Sophie's heart was beating so fast she thought it might burst right out of her chest.

In a fit of anger, Silver grabbed hold of the fireplace and pulled hard to see if it would come away from the wall. He was a powerful man, and it took all of Sienna's strength to hang on to the handle and prevent them from being discovered. When the fireplace didn't move, Silver kicked out at the grate in frustration and moved on to another part of the room.

Just when Sophie thought they might be in the clear, the calf muscle in her right leg went into a sudden cramp. It was agony, but somehow she stopped herself from screaming out in pain. She inhaled sharply, grabbed hold of the toe of her shoe, and pulled it back towards her to relieve the cramp. Silver paused for a moment, believing he had heard a noise. He gestured urgently to his men.

'Shut up, you maggots!' he snapped.

They listened intently for several seconds. It was so quiet, Sophie could hear herself breathing. She screwed up her eyes and pulled hard at the toe of her shoe, and gradually the pain subsided.

When the search of the room proved fruitless, Silver's temper finally got the better of him. He picked up a vase that was sitting on the chest of drawers and flung it against the wall in a raging fury.

'Maybe it's not in the house,' said one of the men. 'Maybe the old man hid it somewhere else.'

Unable to contain his rage, Silver lashed out at the man with a fist, knocking him across the room into the corner.

'Nobody asked for your opinion,' he shouted. The

man said nothing in response. He climbed to his feet and stayed where he was, cowering in the corner and rubbing the side of his face.

'I should burn this old wreck of a house down,' said Silver, his madness now boiling over.

He stormed out onto the landing and pulled down the ladder to the attic, then stamped his way up the steps into the space above them. The other two men followed. Neither of them said another word. It sounded like they were smashing everything that didn't contain the relic. When they came back down to the landing empty-handed, Silver was even more consumed with anger.

'Where is it?' he shouted. 'I'll strangle that old lady when I get my hands on her.'

Sophie felt around for Bunny's hand. When she found it, she gave it a squeeze. Despite the torment she felt from being trapped in such an enclosed space, she was desperate to give her friend a bit of reassurance.

Still shouting threats of violence, Silver thundered back down the stairs, his beleaguered cohorts trailing along behind him. Bunny found it heartbreaking listening to them crashing their way around the house again. It sounded like a wild animal was on the loose. Then everything became silent and still, and a few minutes later there were voices out in the garden. They heard the car start up and the sound of crunching gravel as it made its way down the driveway towards the gates.

A wave of relief flooded through Sophie. Closing her eyes, she exhaled and leaned her head back against the wall. She couldn't wait to push the fireplace door open and step out into the light. But Sienna insisted they should stay in their hiding place until they were sure there was nobody left downstairs. This could be a trap. Silver could still be out there, waiting for them to get careless and show themselves. And if they made a mistake now, it could be fatal.

Chapter 6

It was several minutes before they tentatively pushed the fireplace door open and ventured out into the light. Sienna inched her way across to the bedroom door. The house was eerily silent. Creeping out onto the landing, she headed towards the stairs. But after a few steps, she threw up her hand, halting Sophie and Bunny in their tracks. A little further down, one of the bedroom doors had just moved. They weren't alone in the house after all.

Sophie wondered what was going on. Her mouth was dry, and she was finding it hard to swallow. She unconsciously clenched her fists, ready to do battle, but still not sure what Sienna had seen. In the silent tension, nobody blinked or moved. The only sound they could hear was the ticking of the grandfather clock downstairs in the hallway.

Then Sienna suddenly burst into the room where she had seen the door move, smashing the wooden frame against the internal wall and spinning around to defend herself from attack. The seconds that followed were a frenzy of action. The door jerked away from the wall and a dark shape leapt in Sienna's direction, causing her to lose her balance and be momentarily off guard. She recovered her composure just in time to see Bunny's cat Banjo in full flight. It burst out through the door and rushed down the stairs into the garden.

It was all over in a flash. Sienna exhaled loudly and shook her head in disbelief. When she looked up, Sophie and Bunny were standing by the bedroom door.

'Poor old Banjo,' Bunny whispered. 'Those horrible men must have scared the life out of him.'

They crept through the house, aware that it was still too soon to let their guard down. There was no sign of Silver, but the sight that greeted them in every room caused Bunny to break down in tears. It looked like the house had been hit by a hurricane. Priceless possessions lay broken on the floor, needlessly smashed in anger. Sophie couldn't believe the devastation the men had left behind. She tried to comfort Bunny, but she was inconsolable. First, her beloved Albert had been attacked in the museum, now her home had been ransacked and destroyed.

When Sophie saw the destruction in her bedroom, it made her skin crawl to think the men had been through all of her belongings. Everything had been tipped out of the chest of drawers, and the mattress was lying on its side. She couldn't see her backpack anywhere. She scrabbled around on the floor, digging through the pile of clothes the men had dumped in a big mound on the carpet, but the backpack was nowhere to be seen.

'Oh no, where's the backpack?' she said, desperately searching through the chaos.

'Don't worry,' said Sienna. 'I'm sure it's in here somewhere.'

'No, it's not here. They must have found it. That's probably why they left.'

It was bad enough that Silver had caused such needless damage, but to discover that he had also found the relic was a crushing blow. Sophie was heartbroken. She had promised Albert she wouldn't let the relic fall into the wrong hands, and a day later she had already let him down.

It was only when Sienna started tidying up some of Sophie's clothes that they spotted the strap of the backpack sticking out from under the wardrobe. Sophie rushed across and hurriedly searched inside. It was empty. But when she opened the secret pocket where she had hidden the relic, she was relieved to find that it was still there.

'Oh, thank goodness,' she said, taking the little twist of gold out and placing it on the palm of her hand. 'At least they didn't find the relic.'

'That horrible thing is the reason all of this is happening,' said Bunny, staring at the relic with intense loathing. 'I wish Albert and I had never set eyes on it.'

They set about tidying up the house as best they could. Sophie called out a locksmith to repair the lock on the front door, and they boarded up the gaps where the glass door panels had been destroyed. It took quite a while before things looked anywhere near normal again.

As the afternoon drew to a close, Bunny made a pot of tea and joined the girls in the sitting room with three cups that had survived the men's destructive rampage.

'You're probably wondering why I haven't phoned the police yet,' she said, looking quite fatigued. 'Well, to be honest, it would just mean more disruption, and I don't think I can take any more drama today. And besides, if Albert finds out there's been another break-in, he'll insist on discharging himself from the hospital so he can be here to protect us. And we can't allow that to happen until the doctors say he's well enough to come home.'

Sienna nodded in agreement and inwardly sighed with relief. The last thing she needed was the police asking her questions or investigating anything about her background.

When darkness fell, they kept the lighting low in case Silver was still watching the house. Having already survived one visit from him, they didn't want to do anything that would alert him to their presence. While Bunny was upstairs tidying up her bedroom, Sophie and Sienna sat in the kitchen by the light of a small candle.

'Poor Bunny,' said Sophie. 'Why did those men have to destroy her lovely house?'

'That's how Silver is,' said Sienna. 'As long as he gets what he wants, he doesn't care what happens to anyone else.'

'What was he sent to prison for?' Sophie asked.

'Extortion, blackmail, and conspiracy to murder. At least those are the crimes they found him guilty of. But he's also thought to be responsible for a number of unsolved murders, and several people who opposed his business plans just disappeared.'

'And now he's after the Imperium,' said Sophie. 'Do you think it does actually contain any special powers?'

'I don't know,' said Sienna. 'To be honest, I'm more concerned with finding out where Silver is and making sure he's sent back to The Stockade. He has sworn to take revenge on the senators who sent him to prison, and that committee was led by my father.'

'From what I've heard, your dad is quite capable of looking after himself,' said Sophie, trying to offer her some reassurance.

Sienna smiled back at her. 'That's part of the problem,' she said. 'He thinks he's invincible.'

'So does his daughter,' said Sophie. 'It must be a family tradition.'

They sat and chatted for a while. It was difficult to relax knowing that Silver and his men could appear at any minute. But after the trauma of the afternoon, Sophie was happy just to be in Sienna's company again.

'I wondered what was going on when I saw you coming up the driveway on that motorbike,' said Sophie. 'The visor on your helmet made you look like an android.'

'Yeah, it's not as scary when you find out I'm just a visitor from another world, is it?'

Sophie laughed. She was now so comfortable spending time with Sienna that she didn't think of her as someone from another planet. She was her friend, and the differences between them didn't matter to her.

'This is such an amazing house,' said Sienna. 'How did you end up staying here?'

'Bunny and Albert are friends of my grandparents, and I've been coming here since I was a little girl. So did my mum when she was younger. They're such a lovely couple. It's like having an extra set of grandparents. I hate the idea that something like this could happen to them.'

They heard a noise out in the hallway, and a moment later Bunny appeared at the door holding a piece of paper. She looked drawn and weary. The events of the last twenty-four hours had clearly taken their toll. Sophie pulled out a chair for her, and she joined them at the kitchen table.

'I found this,' said Bunny, placing the piece of paper in the centre of the table. 'It's quite old now, but it's the last address Albert had for T.J. Stapleton. I've been giving all of this some thought, Sophie, and I think you're right. We should warn him. We don't want this to happen to anyone else.'

'Is there a phone number?' Sophie asked.

'No, it's just an address. It's in Winchester, which is about thirty miles east of here. I'll be surprised if there's anyone called Stapleton still living there, but they might be able to give us a forwarding address.'

'I'll go over there on the motorbike first thing tomorrow morning,' said Sienna.

'You're not going without me,' said Sophie. 'Albert wanted me to warn Mr Stapleton, and I'm not going to let him down.'

'Well, whatever you do, I think you girls should stick together,' said Bunny. 'Those men have already shown us what nasty people they are, and I wouldn't be happy if either of you were in the house on your own.'

'In that case, we'll have to find another way to get there,' said Sienna. 'I can't take passengers on the bike until I've passed some sort of test.'

'There's a train,' said Bunny. 'You'd have to change at Southampton, but Winchester is fairly easy to get to from there. I'll be going to the hospital first thing tomorrow morning. If you'd like to stay here tonight, Sienna, I could drop you both at the station on my way over there.'

The girls looked at one another for a moment.

'Thank you, Bunny,' said Sienna, 'that's very kind of you.'

'But what about you?' said Sophie. 'You shouldn't be in the house on your own either.'

'Oh, don't worry about me. I'm hoping they'll let me stay with Albert for most of the day. It's quite a small hospital and the nurses are very kind. And the consultant, Dr Caxton, is a good friend of ours.'

That night, as she lay in bed, Sophie thought about her meeting with Albert the previous afternoon. It was an unusually stilted conversation, and she remembered how on edge he had been. Somehow he must have known those men were coming to the museum, and he wanted to get rid of the relic before they arrived. But why did he give it to her? She knew he was very fond of her, and he would never want to put her life in danger. So he must have had a reason to give her the relic. But what was it?

Chapter 7

The following morning, Sophie woke to the sound of someone rapping firmly on her bedroom door. In the dim light, she could see the outline of Bunny as she swept around the room. She sounded a lot more upbeat than she had been the previous evening.

'Good morning, Sophie,' she trilled. 'It's seven o'clock. Sienna has been up for ages, and I'll have hot pancakes ready in the kitchen in ten minutes.'

Sophie looked out through bleary eyes, then slammed them shut when Bunny drew back the curtains to let in the bright sunlight.

'OK, thank you, Bunny,' she mumbled. 'I'll be right down.'

Breakfast was delicious. Sophie was used to Bunny's generosity, but Sienna was amazed at the feast that was on offer. There were pancakes, fresh fruit, yoghurts and cheeses, and a basket of pastries in case anyone still hadn't had enough. The fridge must have been the only place in the house that the men hadn't ransacked.

'Make sure you eat as much as you can,' said Bunny. 'Breakfast is the most important meal of the day. And you can't be sure when you'll get another chance to eat.'

By eight-thirty, Bunny had dropped the girls at the station and driven off towards the hospital on the other side of the town. It was going to be a long wait for the train. The next service to Southampton wasn't until eight fifty-four.

'I'd suggest going for a cup of tea,' said Sienna, 'but it will be quite a while before I can eat or drink anything else. Bunny really knows how to serve a breakfast, doesn't she? Is she always that generous?'

'Yes, she is,' Sophie answered. 'She and Albert are the most generous people I know. They'd do anything for you.'

'Well, no wonder you rushed into that museum to save Albert from the fire.'

Thinking about the fire again sent Sophie into a cold sweat.

'Don't remind me about that,' she said. 'Just the thought of doing something so reckless still fills me with horror.'

She was expecting Sienna to say something supportive about how brave she had been, but Sienna didn't say a word. Instead, she was looking right past Sophie, her eyes narrowed in concentration.

'Don't turn around,' she said, 'but I think I can see one of those men who came to the house yesterday. He's over at the ticket office.'

Sophie was alarmed to hear that one of Silver's men was in the station. She wanted to spin around, to confirm what Sienna had seen, but somehow she managed to stop herself.

'What's he doing?' she asked.

'He's just standing there. There's no sign of Silver or the other man.'

'Do you think he's following us?'

'Well, if he is, he's doing a terrible job of keeping out of sight.'

A few seconds later, Sophie casually turned around and glanced across at the ticket office. Sienna was right. It was definitely one of the men who had been to the house. He was staring up at the departures board, looking completely baffled. With his thin face, beady eyes, and his wiry and unkempt appearance, Sophie thought he looked like an overgrown rat.

'Let's keep an eye on him and see where he's heading,' said Sienna.

'But what if he's still here when our train arrives? We need to get to Winchester. Mr Stapleton's life could be in danger.'

'Yes, I know,' Sienna answered. 'But my mission is to find out where Silver is, and this idiot might lead us straight to him.'

The man bought himself a takeaway coffee, then looked up at the departures board and wandered across to platform two.

'He's going to platform two,' said Sophie. 'That's where our train comes in.'

'Great,' said Sienna. 'We can follow him over there and see what he does next.'

They crossed over the footbridge to platform two. While they waited, the rat-like man paced up and down, talking to someone on the phone.

'What do we do if he doesn't get on our train?' Sophie asked.

'I'm sorry,' said Sienna, 'but I have to follow him. I might not get another chance like this.'

It was frustrating for Sophie, but she knew that Sienna had no option. This man might lead her straight to Silver. It was too good an opportunity to turn down. Sophie thought about travelling on to Winchester by herself, but she dismissed that idea immediately. After the events of the previous afternoon, she knew it would be much safer if they stuck together.

When the train to Southampton pulled into the station, the rat-like man finished his phone call and stepped through the open doors onto the train. The girls followed him into the carriage and found two seats where they could keep him under surveillance. Sophie thought he looked edgy and ill at ease. While the beautiful English countryside flashed past outside the window, he scrolled through his phone at incredible speed. He never stopped on anything long enough to read it. His mind appeared to be on something else.

Three stops later, he stood up and made his way towards the door. The girls waited until he had stepped off the train, then followed at a safe distance, watching him as he scurried along the platform towards the exit. Even his walking style reminded Sophie of a rat. He scuttled and scampered, and every movement had jerky, nervous energy. At no point did he look around to see if he was being followed. But even if he had, he was unlikely to have suspected two teenage girls of being on his trail.

After winding his way through the streets for about ten minutes, he finally reached the outskirts of the town. The housing had thinned out considerably, and they were approaching the open countryside. Sienna paused for a moment and pulled Sophie behind an overgrown hedge.

'We'd better keep our distance out here,' she said. 'If we get too close to him, he might get suspicious.'

Up ahead of them, the man was now approaching a large area of woodland. He ducked into the trees and disappeared, and by the time the girls reached the wood, he was nowhere to be seen. But a narrow makeshift road ran through the trees, and in the distance, they could see the roof of a secluded house. Sienna didn't want to celebrate too soon, but it was just possible he had led her to Silver's hideout.

'Do you think that's it?' Sophie asked.

'Too early to tell,' said Sienna. 'Let's get a little closer and see what we can find out.'

Under the cover of the trees, they made their way towards the house. Sophie soon realised they were not alone in the wood. The air was alive with birdsong. It reverberated like a sweet wall of sound, muffling the girls' footsteps as they tramped through the undergrowth. When they reached a point where a dappled light broke through the canopy of trees, a dense mass of bluebells stretched out in front of them like a magic blue carpet. It was an uplifting experience that momentarily helped to ease the tension.

It wasn't long before they had a good view of the house. It was a two-storey building with white weatherboards on the upper level and a wide veranda at the back. Sophie thought it could use a bit of love and attention. There was an old van parked outside the front entrance and around to the side a powerful-looking motorbike was up on its stand. And in a garage over at the far side, they could see the black car the men had driven to Abbeville House. Now, at last, Sienna was convinced they had found where Silver was hiding out.

As they peered out from behind a dense thicket of bushes, Sophie could feel her heart pounding away in her chest. The girls had been in a lot of tight situations over the last eight months, and she knew that Sienna would often take massive risks to complete her mission. So what was she planning to do now?

They crouched down and watched the house, hoping to catch a glimpse of Silver. But there was no sign of him anywhere. Sienna took out her phone and got a few photos of the house and the vehicles that were parked outside. Then she turned around and photographed the track that led down to the road.

After a while, a man appeared on the front porch. The girls recognised him instantly as one of the men who had been to Abbeville House. He was tall and overweight, and he had a bruise on the side of his face from where Silver had punched him the previous day. He walked over to the van and grabbed something off the dashboard. As he examined what he had found, Sienna lifted her phone and got a couple of photos of him before he turned and disappeared back through the front door.

'I'll send these to Fraser once we get back to the station,' Sienna whispered. 'They'll be useful if Jutan decides to raid the house.'

They sat and waited, still hoping that Silver might make an appearance, but there was no sign of him. After several minutes, the rat-like man emerged onto the front porch and started walking slowly in their direction. Sophie was terrified that he had spotted them, but as he got closer, she realised that he was unaware they were hiding behind the clump of bushes. He took out his phone, looked over his shoulder towards the house, and tapped a name on his contact list.

'Yeah, he's already got one part of it,' he said, talking in a low voice. 'Now he's determined to get hold of the other two... I don't know. He went to Bournemouth late last night to visit some old archaeologist. The mood he's been in recently, he probably beat the answers out of him... Yeah, he's a bit off the rails right now. I think the time he spent in prison has really pushed him over the edge.'

He was now getting quite close to the girls, but he still seemed to be unaware of their presence. They watched him for a moment, keeping perfectly still. Then Sienna took out her phone to grab another photo to send back to Jutan. But as she touched the screen, the flash on her camera went off accidentally, and the man was suddenly startled into awareness.

'Who's there?' he shouted, rushing towards them. 'Come out of there, right now!'

Sophie's eyes darted towards Sienna. She wondered whether they should turn and run. But it was already too late for that. The rat-like man was standing just a few feet away, and he was pointing a gun straight at them.

Chapter 8

As they stood up to face the man, Sophie thought he was going to shoot them on sight. Her mind was racing and her stomach was in knots. This was going to take a lot of explaining.

'Who are you?' he shouted. 'And why were you taking photos of me?'

The girls had to think quickly, and Sophie said the first thing that came into her head.

'I'm so sorry,' she said. 'We didn't mean any harm. We're from St Dunstan's School in Salisbury, and we're working on a school project.'

'Oh yeah, what's the project? Spying on people?'

His eyes were jerking around frantically. The girls' sudden appearance had clearly unsettled him.

'Put your phones on the ground and back away to that tree,' he shouted, pointing at a large oak tree several feet behind them. 'And leave the backpack there as well.'

Once the girls were a safe distance away, he knelt down and rifled through the backpack. Sophie held her breath, terrified that he would find the secret pocket. To her relief, his search proved fruitless, and he threw the backpack to one side. But when he looked at the phones, it wasn't long before he discovered the photographs Sienna had taken of the men and the house.

'Why have you been taking photos of us?' he barked, stepping forward and pointing the gun at them.

'We're doing a project about people who live in woodland settings,' said Sophie. 'I know we should have asked for your permission first, but we were about to call at the house to let you know what we're doing.'

'Don't lie to me, little girl!' he shouted.

'If you don't believe me, have a look on my phone. There's a message from our geography teacher giving us details of the project. I'll show you if you like.'

She moved towards him, offering to show him on the phone, but he took a few steps back and eyed the girls suspiciously.

'Just tell me where to find it,' he said.

It was only a matter of time before he would discover they were lying, and Sophie knew she couldn't allow that to happen. Aware that Sienna could read her mind, she focused her attention, conjured up a picture of Sienna attacking the man, and hoped Sienna would pick up the image telepathically.

'It's on Gmail,' she said. 'It's from Miss Hobbs.'

All the time Sophie was talking to the man, she was slowly moving away from Sienna. She hoped that if there was a distance between the girls, she could hold his attention and Sienna would get the chance to launch an attack.

'There's nothing here,' said the man.

'No, it's definitely there,' Sophie answered, trying to sound surprised. 'Here, give it to me. Let me show you.'

As she stepped forward, he was momentarily distracted. In the confusion that followed, Sienna saw her chance. She darted forward, desperate to take him down, but before she could get to him he spun around and pointed the gun at her head. It stopped her dead in her tracks.

'Quite aggressive for a couple of schoolgirls on a field trip, aren't you?' he said, looking at Sienna menacingly. 'OK, up to the house. I think my boss might want to have a word with you two.'

Sophie picked up her backpack, and with the rat-like

man following a few paces behind, she trudged dejectedly towards the house. She thought about the relic that was hidden in the secret pocket of her backpack. It was the prize that Silver had attacked Albert for, and now she was taking it right into the heart of his organisation.

They stepped onto the porch and in through the front door.

'Keep walking,' said the rat-like man, 'right down to the end.'

When they passed through the door at the end of the hallway, they found themselves in a large kitchen that opened out onto a veranda. A man was sitting at a wooden table, reading through a pile of papers. It was Silver. He spun around as they entered the room, enraged that they had broken his train of thought.

'Who are these two?' he bellowed, slamming the papers down onto the table.

'I found them snooping around in the woods,' said the rat-like man. 'They've been taking photos of the house. And they've got some of me and Spike as well.'

Silver looked at the girls with a piercing gaze. The icy darkness of his eyes bored into Sophie, and she found it hard to look at him. He stood up and walked over to where they were standing. He was a tall, well-built man with dark hair and a strong jawline. If he had been a less malevolent person, he could have looked almost handsome. But on Silver these features made him seem monstrous and terrifying, and the small scar on his left temple only added to the effect. He towered over the girls, looking to intimidate them with his size.

'Show me the photographs,' he said to the rat-like man.

As she watched Silver scroll through the photos, Sienna knew that they were now in a lot of trouble. Silver didn't play by the usual rules. He was a ruthless killer, and people who had opposed him in the past had simply disappeared, never to be seen again. The girls would have to stick to their story and hope that he believed them. If he didn't, they may never get out of the house alive.

'They claim the photos are for a school project,' said the rat-like man. 'They say they're studying people who live in woodland settings. But if you ask me—'

'Nobody is asking you,' said Silver.

He looked at the girls in silence for several seconds. Sophie felt as if his eyes were burrowing into her soul. When she glanced over at Sienna, she was surprised by how uncharacteristically nervy she looked. Silver's intimidating presence had shaken her usual steely resolve.

'I know you from somewhere, don't I?' said Silver, taking a step closer to Sienna.

Sienna shook her head, trying to look casual. 'No, I don't think so,' she said. 'I'm not from around here. I live in Salisbury.'

'And what about you?' said Silver, turning suddenly to Sophie, and glaring at her with menace in his eyes.

Sophie swallowed hard. She hadn't been expecting his question, and initially, she was too flustered to answer.

'Erm,' she muttered eventually. 'I'm from Salisbury too. We're doing a geography project for school. We're sorry to have disturbed you.'

He reached forward and grabbed the backpack from her shoulder, taking her by surprise and causing her to gasp involuntarily. As he rummaged his hand around inside, the girls watched in silence, aware that they were a fingertip away from disaster. His search seemed to take forever. When he found nothing, he threw it back at her aggressively, and she slipped the backpack onto her shoulder again.

Nobody said anything for a moment. Silver appeared to be deep in thought. Then he turned and stared intently at Sienna.

'You're both lying,' he said, 'but I'm not sure why.'

He held Sienna's gaze for a few more seconds. Finally, he turned to the rat-like man who was nervously awaiting instructions.

'Lock them in the basement until I decide what to do with them,' he said, before returning to the table to carry on reading through the pile of papers.

The rat-like man marched the girls out into the hallway and pulled open the door that led down to the basement.

'Downstairs,' he said, pointing the gun at the open doorway.

A rickety old staircase led down into the darkness. It was poorly lit, and as the girls made their way downstairs, they heard the rat-like man locking the door behind them. Their situation now looked desperate. They were trapped in a gloomy basement at the mercy of a dangerous criminal, and they knew that nobody was coming to rescue them.

The basement was dank and squalid, and what little light there was came from a small, rectangular window high up at the top of one of the walls. It was quite a large space with a pool table down at one end and two battered old sofas running along the far wall. The window let in a bit of light, but it didn't let in anywhere near enough air to deal with the musty smell.

Any optimism Sophie felt at the start of the day had now completely vanished. She had only been in Silver's presence for a short time, but it was long enough to know that they were now in serious danger. She slumped down onto one of the sofas and stared at the ground despondently.

'We've got to get out of here,' said Sienna, her eyes darting around the room. She crossed over to the wall and tried to pull herself up to the window, but it was just a little too high.

'Help me drag that sofa over here,' she said. 'With a bit of luck, we might be able to squeeze through there.'

They hauled the battered sofa over to the window. But when Sienna stood on the back of it and tried to push her head through the gap, she gave up almost immediately.

'It's too small,' she said, kicking the wall in frustration. She dropped down onto the old sofa and sat there, deep in thought.

'There has to be another way out,' she said. 'I'm not waiting down here while he decides how to dispose of us.'

They had only been in the basement for a few minutes when they heard the key turning in the door. Several seconds later, the rat-like man appeared at the bottom of the stairs.

'Right,' he said, pointing a gun at them. 'Get yourselves back upstairs. Mr Silver wants a word with you.'

Sophie picked up her backpack, and the girls traipsed up the stairs to the kitchen. Silver was still sitting at the table, but he was looking a lot more relaxed than when they had encountered him earlier. There was a large, brown envelope on the table in front of him.

'Take a seat,' he said, pointing at the two chairs directly opposite him.

The girls hesitated for a moment before pulling out the chairs and sitting down.

'Will this take long?' said Sienna, determined to appear unconcerned. 'We've got to be back at school by lunchtime.'

Silver didn't respond. He fixed her with an evil stare and leaned back in his chair.

'As you've dropped in so unexpectedly,' he said, 'I

thought I'd tell you a story. It's a success story, showing that no matter what life throws at you, if you remain steadfast good fortune will always come to your aid.'

'Oh good,' said Sienna. 'I like a happy ending.'

It lifted Sophie's spirits to see Sienna's belligerent attitude, but Silver was unfazed by her response. He carried on with his story as if she hadn't spoken.

'It's a story about a young man who had a vision of greatness. Despite his humble beginnings, he set his sights on a glittering future, and he worked every minute that he could to achieve that ambition. His rise through the ranks of society was meteoric, and soon he was rubbing shoulders with the high and mighty. He had position and power, and he was setting his sights on even greater glory.'

Sienna eyed him carefully. Having read through the files that Jutan gave her, she could already tell where this story was heading.

'But the high and mighty didn't enjoy having to mix with this interloper,' Silver continued. 'His ambition frightened them, and they found a way to bring him to heel. Crimes were invented, charges were brought, and soon our hero had been locked away in The Stockade, a prison from which no one had ever escaped.'

'I thought you said this story had a happy ending,' said Sienna, staring back at him unflinchingly.

'But the story has only just begun,' said Silver. 'The Stockade couldn't hold our hero. No prison could. He escaped with the help of the few friends he had left, and he set about plotting his revenge on those who had unjustly locked him away.'

'Oh good,' said Sienna, 'we're getting to the exciting part.'

Silver rubbed his chin and smiled back at her. It was a chilling smile. It put Sophie in mind of a snake.

'Yes,' said Silver. 'It's the exciting part. And there are plenty of twists and turns yet to come.'

As he carried on with his story, Sophie was feeling more and more uncomfortable. She had a feeling she wouldn't like how this story ended.

'All the time our hero was in exile,' Silver continued, 'he was driven by the promise of revenge on one man; the man who had sentenced him to spend his life in The Stockade. He kept a photograph of that man to fuel his thirst for revenge and to remind him he must never forget this injustice. Would you like to see it?'

'Do we have a choice?' Sienna asked.

'No,' Silver answered. He looked almost jubilant, as if he couldn't wait to unveil his prize.

Picking up the brown envelope, he pulled out its contents and placed a large photograph down on the table in front of them. Sienna was expecting to be confronted with bad news, but she hadn't prepared herself for anything as challenging as this. There on the table was the smiling face of her father, Memphis. And standing next to him was his teenage daughter, Sienna.

'I was wondering how I could gain an advantage in my plan to avenge my incarceration,' said Silver. 'And it seems good fortune has smiled upon me once again, by sending me the best bargaining chip I could have hoped for.'

'My father would never bargain with vermin like you,' said Sienna, looking to hide her inner turmoil.

Silver narrowed his eyes and smiled his reptilian smile.

'I will give your father an ultimatum,' he said. 'Surrender to my authority so I may pass judgment on him as he did on me, or his daughter will die a slow and agonising death.'

He turned to the rat-like man who was standing by the window.

'Take them down to the basement,' he said. 'And make sure the door is securely locked.'

Chapter 9

Sienna felt a heavy weight on her shoulders as she trudged back down to the basement. By allowing herself to be caught by Silver, she had put her father's life in danger, and she was devastated that she had also dragged Sophie into such a life-threatening situation.

'We have to find a way out of here,' she said, anxiously pacing up and down. 'I can't allow my father to surrender to Silver. It would mean certain death for him.'

Sophie stared back at her, looking ashen-faced. Now that Silver had discovered Sienna's identity, she thought their position looked hopeless.

'What do you think he's going to do with us?' she asked.

'I don't know,' said Sienna. 'I'm not waiting around to find out, though. Silver may have painted us a nice romantic picture of his life. But in reality, he is a ruthless criminal who has been responsible for the deaths of countless innocent people. That's why the committee sent him to The Stockade.'

She scoured the basement for anything that could help them escape, opening cupboard doors and crouching down to look under the furniture.

'There must be something in here that we could use to help us get out,' she said.

'What are we looking for?' Sophie asked.

'I'm not sure,' said Sienna. 'I'm hoping we'll see something and it will spark an idea.'

Sophie scrabbled around inside the backpack, wondering if there were any paperclips or hairgrips lurking down at the bottom. She knew that Sienna was an expert at lock picking, and with the right tools she could get the door at the top of the stairs open. But her search proved fruitless. She dropped the backpack onto the sofa and slumped down beside it despondently.

'No luck?' Sienna asked.

'I'm afraid not. I was hoping I might have a few paperclips, so you could do your lock-picking thing.'

At the mention of picking the lock, Sienna's eyes lit up with excitement. She had assumed they would have to fight their way out of the house, but maybe Sophie had just given them a more subtle route.

'Is it alright if I take a look through that backpack?' Sienna asked. 'There might be something else in there that we could use.'

She searched through the backpack and pulled out a ball-point pen, then took the ink cartridge out and examined it carefully.

'You know what? I think this might work,' she said, slipping the cartridge into her pocket. 'Now all we have to do is get past those three freaks upstairs.'

Finding the ink cartridge filled Sienna with renewed optimism. She climbed onto the back of the sofa and peered out through the rectangular window, to check how things were on the outside. The rat-like man was at the front of the house. He was leaning over the engine of the van, holding a pair of pliers. There was no sign of Silver or the other man.

'OK,' she said. 'One of them is working at the front of the house, so if we pick the lock we won't be able to go out through the front door. We'll have to hope there's nobody in the kitchen so we can go out the back way. If it all goes to plan, we can head into the woods. It should be easy to hide out there for a while. Then, once everything dies down, we can head back into town.'

They crept up to the top of the stairs and listened at the door for a few moments. When they were sure there was nobody outside, Sienna knelt down and pushed the plastic end of the ink cartridge into the lock. For several minutes she wiggled it around, hoping it would latch onto something and trigger the lock. But she was out of luck. She sat back on her heels, shaking her head in frustration.

'Looks like this won't be as easy as I thought,' she said in a soft voice.

'Well, there doesn't seem to be any other way out,' Sophie whispered, 'so we might as well keep trying.'

Before Sienna could respond, someone entered the house through the front door. The girls listened in silence as footsteps scuttled down the hall. It sounded like the rat-like man. He scurried past the door to the basement, heading towards the kitchen. The fridge door opened. A few seconds later, it slammed shut. Then the footsteps headed out into the hall again.

Sophie held her breath and kept perfectly still, hoping he had just called in for some liquid refreshment. But when he reached the door to the basement, he paused for a moment. The door handle turned, and the door rattled hard against the lock.

The girls didn't know what to do. They couldn't rush back down the stairs. The sound of their boots on the rickety wooden steps would definitely have given them away. Their only option was to stay where they were and hope he was just checking the door was still locked. The handle turned again, and the door rattled against the lock. Then the footsteps carried on down the hall and out through the front door onto the porch. Sophie leaned her head back against the wall and gave a massive sigh of relief.

'Wow, that was close,' she whispered.

Once they were sure the hallway was empty, Sienna crouched down again and pushed the plastic end of the cartridge back into the lock. She rocked it back and forth in an anti-clockwise direction, listening for any sounds of movement. It was slow going. Sophie tried to stay calm, but she could tell that Sienna was becoming impatient. The process seemed to take forever. Finally, after a few more minutes, they heard the soft clunk of the lock, and Sienna turned the handle and inched the door open a little. There was nobody around. She looked at Sophie and smiled.

'Second time lucky,' she whispered. 'Let's get out of here.'

They eased the door open and crept out into the hallway. It was so quiet that Sophie was frightened to breathe. When they peered in through the kitchen door, they could see Silver out on the veranda, still going through his paperwork. Fortunately, he was sitting with his back to them so they could move around unseen. But they would have to find another way out of the house.

Creeping along the hallway, they stopped just before the door of the sitting room. At the far side of the room, they could see the overweight man lying on his back, asleep on a sofa. Sophie thought he looked like a beached whale. Sienna pointed to a small study a little further down. The door was wide open, and through the window, they could see the woods at the side of the house. They both knew at once that this could be their escape route.

It was a small room with a large wooden desk and shelves running along one wall that were overflowing with books. The girls' phones were sitting on the desk, and next to them were a third phone, two motorcycle helmets and a set of keys. They grabbed their phones and slipped them into their pockets. Then Sienna picked up the third phone and examined it.

'Sienna, let's go,' Sophie whispered. 'There isn't time for this.'

Much as she hated to admit it, Sienna knew that Sophie was right. She slipped the third phone into Sophie's backpack, then crept across the room to the window. There didn't appear to be anyone outside. It would only be a short dash to the woods. But when she tried to open the window, it was so stiff she could only get it to move a few inches. Sienna hadn't bargained for this.

She grabbed hold of the frame again and put every ounce of strength into getting it open. It didn't budge at all. Taking a deep breath, she tried again. This time it flew open with a resounding crash and Sophie's heart leapt into her mouth. For an agonising few seconds, the girls held their breath, listening out for Silver and his men. But nobody came. They climbed through the window and crouched down by the side of the house.

'Let's take the bike,' Sienna whispered, pointing to the powerful motorcycle that was standing a few feet away.

Sophie stared back at her, open-mouthed in shock.

'Come on,' Sienna whispered. 'The helmets and keys are on that desk.'

'But they'll hear us starting it up. Wouldn't it be better if we just crept off into the woods?'

'If we take the bike, we could be away from here in a

flash,' Sienna answered. 'By the time they're able to react, we'll be long gone.'

She climbed back through the window, grabbed the helmets and keys off the desk, then ducked out and handed a helmet to Sophie.

'It was nice of them to leave those there for us,' she whispered, pulling on her helmet.

Sophie still wasn't convinced, but she could tell that Sienna was in no mood to argue. She dragged the helmet onto her head, jumped onto the back of the bike and found something solid to hold on to. Sienna turned to her and smiled.

'Hold on tight,' she whispered. 'This could be a wild ride.' Then she pulled down the visor of her helmet and fired up the ignition.

As soon as the engine sprang into life, Sienna let out the throttle, and the motorbike burst from the side of the house onto the makeshift track that ran down to the main road. When the rat-like man saw them flash past, he threw down his tools and attempted to give chase, but they were already halfway down the track.

'Hey!' he shouted. 'Come back here, you little brats.'

Seconds later, Silver and the overweight man appeared on the front porch.

'It's those girls,' said the rat-like man. 'They've stolen the bike.'

Silver was incandescent with rage. He grabbed the rat-like man by the collar and threw him against the side of the van.

'I thought I told you to lock them in the basement,' he shouted. 'If they get away, I'm going to make you wish you'd never been born. Now get in the van and get after them, you idiot!'

Chapter 10

The two men jumped into the van and sped off down the track, with Silver right behind them in the black car. On the uneven, makeshift road, the old van rattled and crashed around, but the rat-like man drove it forward relentlessly. Having seen how Silver dealt with people who had let him down in the past, he had no intention of experiencing the same fate.

Up ahead of him, the girls were almost at the end of the track. It was a bumpy ride, and Sienna wasn't used to handling such a powerful motorcycle. It took enormous concentration to keep the bike upright as she dodged around the ruts and potholes. She gritted her teeth, determined to stay focused. One mistake and their escape plan would come crashing to the ground.

When they reached the main road, Sienna opened up the throttle, and they headed out into the open countryside. The bike was now moving at tremendous speed. Sophie was shocked at how exposed and vulnerable they were. She had been on the back of her Uncle John's motorbike on several occasions, but pottering around the town on his tiny bike was nowhere near as terrifying as this. She clung on in desperation, hoping and praying that Sienna knew what she was doing.

The wind battered against them as they tore down the open road. When Sienna looked in the rear-view mirror, she could see that the van and the black car were hot on their trail. Over the roar of the bike's engine, they heard a gunshot. She looked in her wing mirror again, and she could tell that the van was gaining on them. Sienna didn't know whether she dare go any faster. At times she didn't feel totally in control. But she knew that the longer they could keep the bike on the road, the more chance they would have of shaking off their pursuers.

They powered past a broken-down old farm building, scattering sheep in a nearby field. It was a good thing that the road was so clear. The slightest delay and their getaway could have turned to disaster. Another shot rang out. It shattered the off-side wing mirror, spraying them with fragments of glass that battered against their helmets like a hailstorm.

Road signs flashed past at regular intervals, but Sienna was so focused on eluding Silver that she barely noticed them. If she had, she would have realised they were approaching a humpback bridge, and at the speed they were travelling they could be heading for a catastrophe.

They were on the bridge before the girls knew what was happening. When they hit the hump, the bike launched into the air and hung there for a moment before slamming down onto the road on the other side. Sophie was almost jolted out of her seat. She let out a yelp of terror and grabbed at the strap of her backpack to stop it from slipping off her shoulder. The bike wobbled alarmingly and lurched over to the other side of the road. Sienna thought they were going down. But they were travelling so fast, the forward momentum helped her to keep it under control.

Almost immediately, they heard a crashing sound as the van took the humpback bridge and slammed back down onto the road again. Silver and his men were still in hot pursuit. Nothing Sienna did could shake them off. Another shot rang out. It whistled past them into the road beyond. The men were closing in on them, and it was only a matter of time before one of the bullets hit its target.

Up ahead, Sienna could see a temporary traffic light. The road had narrowed to a single lane while one side of the road was being repaired. The light was against them, but there was no way Sienna was going to stop. She powered through the red light, causing a car that was heading towards her to brake suddenly and the driver to lean on the horn in anger. Seconds later, the van and the black car ploughed through the lights after her. The oncoming car had to swerve violently and ended up on the grass verge at the side of the road.

Silver and his men were now so close that Sienna thought she might have to take drastic action. But when they came out of the next bend, she gasped with horror and her heart nearly leapt into her mouth. A large tractor was pulling out of a field, and it was hauling a trailer filled with farming equipment.

It was too late for Sienna to slam on the brakes. They were travelling too fast and braking suddenly could have sent the girls somersaulting to the ground. The tractor was taking up most of the road, so her only chance was to go for the gap on the far side and hope there was enough room for her to squeeze the bike through. She gave it more throttle as a last roll of the dice, put her head down and headed for the tiny gap.

Sophie was now convinced she was about to die. As the foliage from the roadside bushes lashed against her arm, she closed her eyes and tensed every muscle, hoping that their luck would hold. When they hit the uneven ground at the edge of the road, the bike vibrated violently, and Sienna had to strain every sinew to keep it under control. She clenched her jaw and let out a strangulated cry. Then keeping her eyes fixed on a spot further down the road, she squeezed through the gap and out onto the open road at the other side.

The men in the van weren't so fortunate. By the time the rat-like man came around the bend, the tractor was blocking up the entire road. There was no way for him to get past. He slammed on the brakes and the van went into a violent spin, smashing sideways into the trailer and catapulting across the road. It rolled over several times before careering off the road and ending up in a ditch.

As Sienna powered away from the scene of the accident, they could hear the squealing of brakes and the smashing together of the vehicles as the van ploughed into the trailer. It was a sickening sound of mangled metal and shattering glass, and a stark reminder of how close the girls had come to disaster.

A little further down the road, Sienna pulled over to the grass verge, and the girls looked back at the carnage they had left behind. The van was lying upside down in the ditch with its wheels still spinning. The windscreen had shattered, and one of the doors had been ripped off its hinges. There was no sign of either of the men.

Beyond the accident, they could see the black car. It had pulled over to the side of the road and Silver was standing beside it, looking past the wreckage towards the girls. Even from this distance, his eyes seemed to bore right into Sophie. He didn't move. He just stood there, staring at them menacingly. It was chilling to see how unconcerned he was about his men.

Sophie flipped up the visor of her helmet.

'I can't believe he isn't going to help them,' she said. 'They could be badly injured.'

'Silver never thinks about anyone but himself,' said Sienna. 'To him, they're just numbers. He doesn't care whether they live or die.'

By now the farmer had climbed down from the cab of his tractor and rushed over to where the van was lying in a ditch. He didn't appear to be seriously injured. The trailer must have taken the full force of the crash. But when he slid down the bank into the ditch and looked through the window of the van, he obviously didn't like what he saw. He scrambled back up to the road, pulled out his phone and hurriedly punched in some numbers.

'He's probably calling for an ambulance,' said Sophie.

'In that case, we'd better get out of here,' said Sienna. 'The police could be here at any minute, and I can't afford to get involved with them.'

As they pulled onto the road again, Sophie turned and looked back towards the scene of the accident. The black car had already gone. Silver had abandoned his men to their fate. They had served their purpose, and it was time for him to move on to more important things. The brutality of it left Sophie feeling shell-shocked and nauseated. Clinging on to the back of the bike, she wondered what the rest of the day would bring. Today was supposed to be an investigative journey, a chance to do a bit of sleuthing as they tried to track down T.J. Stapleton. But after a hair-raising bike ride to escape from a ruthless killer, she knew they were lucky to still be alive. Good fortune had been on their side, but for how much longer would it last?

Chapter 11

They headed towards the next town, moving at a more conventional speed this time. Sophie was happy to travel in silence. She was still reeling from the events of the morning, and she was glad to have some time to process it all. She thought about Silver and wondered why he had disappeared from the scene of the accident so quickly. Had he circled around and found another way onto this road? Could he be waiting for them a little further down? Her mind was filled with a strange sense of foreboding as if the greatest threat to their lives was still to come.

As they cruised through the open countryside, Sienna was unaware of Sophie's inner turmoil. She felt invigorated by their escape, and she was enjoying the thrill of riding such a powerful machine. Uplifted by the experience, her exposure to the elements enhanced every sound and smell. The noise of the wind, the fragrance of the spring flowers — it all sent her senses into overdrive.

After a few uneventful minutes, they passed an ambulance moving in the opposite direction. Several seconds later, a police car followed with its siren blaring. Sophie thought about the men who had been following them in the van. Despite their malicious intent, she hoped they hadn't been seriously injured.

When they reached the town, Sienna pulled into a large car park and brought the bike to a halt in an empty bay. She took off her helmet and shook out her hair, then hung the helmet on the handlebars and turned to face Sophie.

'Much as I'd love to ride this thing around all day,' she said, 'I think we should leave it here and walk the rest of the way to the station. I don't think it's that far.'

Sophie didn't need to be persuaded. She climbed off the bike and left the helmet on the seat. It was a big relief to have both feet firmly back on solid ground.

Crossing over to the other side of the car park, they followed the signposts for the station. It was a busy morning in the town, and the rich aromas drifting out of the pavement cafes reminded Sophie that they hadn't eaten for some time. She dug around in her backpack and found two cereal bars that Bunny had insisted she take with her.

'Would you like one of these?' she said, offering a bar to Sienna.

'What is it?' Sienna asked.

'It's a cereal bar. I know it looks like it was scraped off the floor of a hamster's cage and mashed up together, but they actually taste quite good.'

Sienna peeled back the wrapping and took a bite. She nodded to Sophie as she continued to chew.

'Not bad,' she said. 'It tastes a lot better than it looks.'

On reaching the next road junction, they paused for a moment while they waited for the lights to change. Sophie looked over to the other side of the road. There was a white van in the queue of traffic with two men in the driver's compartment. She thought about the accident they had left behind and wondered what had happened to Silver's henchmen.

'Do you think those two men who were chasing us will be alright?' she asked.

'I can't say I'm bothered either way,' said Sienna.

Sophie was a little shocked by Sienna's reply.

'I know they were shooting at us,' she said, 'but they didn't deserve to die.'

'If they'd run the bike off the road, do you think they'd be having the same conversation about us?'

'Well, no,' said Sophie, 'but that doesn't mean we have to be like them.'

They crossed the road and walked in silence for a while.

'You enjoyed riding that bike, didn't you?' Sophie asked. 'I couldn't believe it when you tried to squeeze past the tractor.'

'To be honest, I didn't have any choice,' said Sienna. 'We were going so fast that if I'd tried anything else, it could have been a disaster.' Then she turned to Sophie and smiled. 'But yes, I loved riding that bike.'

'I wish I could be like you sometimes,' said Sophie.

'What do you mean?'

'Well, you just act, don't you? You don't worry about the odds or think about the consequences. You just go for it. You saw the bike, and you took it. You saw the gap left by the tractor, and you went for it.'

'Sometimes there isn't time to think,' said Sienna. 'Seconds count, and you have to trust your instincts and just make things happen. That's what you did when you saved Albert from the fire. If you'd given yourself time to think about it, he might not have survived.'

'Don't remind me about the fire,' said Sophie. 'I can't believe how reckless that was.'

'You weren't reckless; you were decisive. What you did that night was very brave.'

'I could have been killed.'

'But you weren't,' said Sienna. 'You were heroic. You unleashed that noble and courageous part of yourself that's usually crowded out by your rational mind.'

Sophie paused and thought about what Sienna had said.

'But our rational minds are a good thing, aren't they?' she said. 'They give us the ability to think things through.'

'All I'm saying is, if you think about things for too long, you'll never do anything. You can always find a reason for playing safe. And what kind of life is that?'

'A safe one?' said Sophie, smiling back at her.

'Or a boring one,' said Sienna. 'Your uncle John once told me of a saying in your world. "It's better to live for one day as a tiger than a thousand years as a sheep." I like that.'

'And how does that apply to me?'

'Well, when you realised Albert was stuck inside the burning museum, the tiger in you overpowered your rational mind and your true spirit just acted. It was one of those glorious moments in life when we experience who we truly are.'

Sophie found it disturbing to hear this about herself. She hated being out of control, and the idea that she would act without thinking filled her with horror. But Sienna was right. That's what she did on the night of the fire, and it was the only reason that Albert was still alive.

It didn't take long to find the station and, despite being quite a small town, it was a relief to find there was a regular service to Southampton. From there it would only be another seventeen minutes to Winchester.

While they waited for the train, Sophie had the nagging feeling that they were being followed. It was an unnerving experience. Every time she looked up, a man on a nearby bench appeared to be watching them. When he caught Sophie's eye, he would look away for a moment before glancing over again when he thought she wasn't looking. Finally, after a few uncomfortable minutes, he moved down to the other end of the platform.

Sienna was oblivious to the man's presence. She was busy examining the phone they took from Silver's house, hoping it would give an insight into his plans. But she couldn't find anything that seemed significant. As there was still some time before the train arrived, she decided to send the phone to Jutan so it could be examined in more detail.

They found a post office a few doors down from the station, slipped the phone into a padded envelope, and posted it to an address that Fraser had given Sienna the previous day. Then she sent him an email, attached the photographs of Silver's house and confirmed that it was Silver who set fire to the Abbeville House museum.

They got back to the station with only seconds to spare and jumped onto the train just as the guard was blowing his whistle. It didn't take long to reach Winchester. Soon Sophie was consulting the map on her phone, trying to work out how to get to the address that Bunny had given them. The house appeared to be only a ten-minute walk away, not far from the historic cathedral that the beautiful city was famous for.

The crispness of the morning had long since gone, and it had warmed up into a glorious spring day. Sophie took off her jacket and slung it over her shoulder, glad to feel the warmth of the sun again. All around them, the well-kept gardens were awash with beautiful spring flowers. At one point they passed a cherry blossom tree that was in full bloom. Its beautiful white flowers carpeted the ground like discarded confetti. Finally, when she thought they were close to their destination, Sophie took out her phone and had another look at the map.

'I think that's it,' she said, pointing to a well-kept detached property a little further down.

The house was a beautiful Victorian villa with a large garden at the front and an ornately tiled pathway that led to the front door. At either side of the door, there was a large pot housing a bay tree. Everything about the house was immaculate.

They pushed the front gate open and walked up the winding path towards the house. The garden was still recovering from the bleakness of winter, but whoever lived there was clearly a fan of spring flowers. Daffodils and tulips were dotted around in a variety of different shades, and several other plants looked as if they were about to burst into life.

Sienna rang the doorbell, and they heard it chime inside the house. But there was no response. They waited for about a minute, then she tried the bell again. There was still no sign of anyone.

'He's probably out,' said Sophie. 'Perhaps we should come back later.'

'Or maybe someone else beat us to it,' said Sienna,

'and Stapleton has met the same fate as Albert.'

On hearing Sienna's words, Sophie became a little panicked. She peered through the glass panels on the front door, but the frosting on the glass made it difficult to make out any shapes.

'Let's go around to the back,' said Sienna. 'There might be a window or a door open.'

'Now hang on, Sienna. We're not thinking of breaking in, are we?'

'Of course not,' Sienna answered, looking the other way. 'I just want to check if there's anything odd going on.'

The back garden was just as well tended as the front, with a host of flowers and shrubs that had been awakened by the arrival of spring. Sophie peered in through the kitchen window, but there was no sign of anyone inside. When they reached the French doors that led out onto the patio, Sienna tried the handle to see if the door was open. Sophie was about to caution her against doing anything illegal when, out of the corner of her eye, she noticed some movement over her right shoulder.

When she turned around, a large brown dog was standing just outside the door of a shed. Its body looked muscular and powerful, and it was emitting a low growl and baring its teeth. Sophie froze with terror at the sight of it. She had a lifelong fear of dogs, and this one was big enough to overpower a large adult. She swallowed hard. Her feet felt like concrete. The dog was moving slowly towards them, and it looked like it was about to attack.

Chapter 12

For a few seconds, Sophie just stood there, unable to move or speak. She was so frozen to the spot that she was barely breathing. Then, taking a step back, she finally squeezed out a few words.

'Erm, Sienna,' she muttered, keeping her eyes on the dog.

When Sienna turned around, she was just as alarmed by the size of the dog. She crept across to where Sophie stood, reached out, and took hold of her arm. This was not the time for heroics. She knew they had to get out of the garden right away.

'OK,' she said. 'Let's slowly back out of here. That looks like a really angry dog.'

But as they moved away to the side of the house, the dog sprang forward and blocked off their exit. Snarling and baring its razor-sharp teeth, it defiantly stood in their way.

'Steady Aslan!' a man's voice shouted. 'Step back! Now!'

An elderly man appeared from out of the shed. He walked over to where the dog was still growling at the girls and took it by the collar.

'Sit down!' he commanded. The dog sat down with the man still holding on to its collar. It had stopped growling, but it was still looking at them menacingly.

'Oh hello,' said Sienna, trying to pretend that everything was quite normal. 'We're looking for Mr Stapleton.'

'It's customary to knock on someone's front door when you first visit their house,' said the man, eyeing them suspiciously.

'Oh yes, we rang the doorbell,' said Sophie, 'but there was no answer.'

'At that point, most normal people would go away and maybe come back later,' the man replied.

'Yes, of course,' said Sophie, looking nervously from the man to the dog and back again.

'But you decided to sneak around the back and see if the door was open.'

'Look, I know this doesn't look good,' said Sienna, 'but we need to talk to Mr Stapleton urgently.'

'I don't know anyone called Stapleton,' said the man.

'T.J. Stapleton? The archaeologist?' said Sophie. 'He used to live here. We wondered if he'd left a forwarding address.'

'Why do you want to speak to him?'

'We think his life might be in danger,' said Sienna.

'And what makes you think that?'

'We're friends of Bunny and Albert Robson,' said Sophie. 'Someone attacked Albert the other night, and we think the same person may be after Mr Stapleton.'

The man paused for a few seconds. 'What happened to Albert?' he said, finally.

'He was attacked in his museum late at night,' Sophie answered, 'and whoever did it set fire to the museum and left Albert to die. Fortunately, we were able to get him out before the fire really took hold, but he's still in hospital.'

The man paused again. He let go of the dog's collar and motioned towards the house.

'You'd better come inside,' he said.

He took a key out of his pocket and unlocked the back door, stepping aside to let the girls in. The dog trotted in behind them. Its initial aggression seemed to have faded. Inside, there was a large kitchen table with four chairs around it.

'Take a seat,' said the man.

When Sophie sat down at the table, the dog walked over and sat on the floor by her chair. The man looked at the dog, then studied Sophie for a moment. He took some cups out of the cupboard and put a tea-bag into each of them. As he waited for the kettle to boil, he stood at the end of the table and looked directly at Sophie.

'OK,' he said, 'tell me your story.'

'My name is Sophie Watson, and this is my friend Sienna.' The man didn't even look at Sienna but kept his eyes on Sophie. She found it a little unsettling.

'We're staying at Abbeville House at the moment because my mum and dad are abroad.'

'Why Abbeville House?' the man asked. 'Are you Bunny and Albert's granddaughter?'

'No, we're not related, but Bunny and Albert have always been like grandparents to me. Two nights ago, there was a fire at the museum and Albert was lucky to escape alive. The police and fire service think it was started deliberately, and that Albert may have been attacked.'

'And what has Albert had to say about this?'

'Nothing yet,' said Sophie. 'The police haven't been able to interview him because the blow he took to the head has left him a little confused.'

The man took a moment to consider Sophie's story, then walked over to the just-boiled kettle and made three cups of tea. Once he had passed the tea around, he stood looking at Sophie, cradling his cup in his hands.

'OK,' he said, continuing to ignore Sienna. 'I'll tell you what I know. Normally I try to get rid of strangers who come around here with their stories. I've been conned too many times in the past. But the dog seems to trust you. And dogs are a better judge of a person than I'll ever be.'

He took a sip of his tea, then put it down on the table.

'I'm not Stapleton, and I don't think he has ever lived here. I've owned this house for over thirty years, and the woman I bought it off was a doctor who had retired and was moving away to Cornwall. I am an archaeologist, but I'm sorry to tell you I don't know any archaeologists called Stapleton.'

'T.J. Stapleton?' said Sophie, hopefully. 'We think he used to work with Albert in the 1960s.'

'Well, now you're going back a bit,' said the man. 'I know I look old, but that's a little before my time. I know Bunny and Albert, though. Not well, but I've met them a few times over the years. They're good people, and I'm sorry to hear about what's happened to Albert. Do you know whether anything was taken from the museum?'

'I'm afraid not,' said Sophie. 'Bunny thinks the attack may be connected to a Mayan tomb that Herbert Hawkins discovered somewhere in Guatemala.'

'Ah yes. I've read about that expedition, and I know all the legends about what Hawkins discovered in the tomb. But I'm afraid I couldn't tell you any more than you could find out on the internet.'

'Oh,' said Sophie. 'Well, we're sorry to have bothered you then.'

'You should try the British Museum.'

'The British Museum?' said Sophie.

'Yes, when I was there last month, I'm sure I saw something about that dig in a glass case in the American history section. Other than that, I don't know what to suggest.'

'OK, thank you,' said Sophie. 'We might check that out.'

They finished their tea and stood up to leave.

'I hope Albert's OK,' said the man. 'Please send my regards to Bunny and Albert. My name is James Adamson.'

'Thank you, Mr Adamson. I'll do that.'

They walked towards the front door; the dog staying close to Sophie throughout.

'There's one other thing you should know,' said Mr Adamson. 'Someone else has been here, asking about that dig. He was a tall man with a small scar on the side of his head. Does that ring any bells?'

Sienna's eyes widened when she heard the description, but she said nothing.

'No, I can't say that it does,' Sophie answered.

'I told him nothing. I wouldn't even let him into the house. The dog didn't like him, you see. Never stopped growling all the time he was on the doorstep. Dogs can spot a wrong 'un a mile off.'

Chapter 13

As they trudged back through the streets of Winchester, Sophie struggled to understand why Bunny had sent them to Mr Adamson's house. If she and Albert had any sort of friendship with James Adamson, surely she would have known that it was his address.

'So what do we do now?' she said, feeling a little dejected. She had been hoping to find T.J. Stapleton, or at least get some information on where they could contact him. But now they seemed to be further away from finding him than ever.

'How far is it to that museum?' Sienna asked.

'The British Museum? It's in central London, so it would take quite a while to get there.'

Sienna was undeterred. 'We should still check it out, though,' she said. 'After all, it's the only lead we have.'

They pressed on towards the station, going over every

detail of their conversation with Mr Adamson.

'It's strange that he has never heard of T.J. Stapleton, isn't it?' said Sophie, as they approached the outside of the station.

'Yes. You think they'd have come across one another at some point. And that was definitely Silver who called at his house. Why did you tell Mr Adamson you didn't recognise his description?'

'Well, what could I have said? Oh yes, I know him. He's from another world, and he's looking for the relics so he can become all-powerful and wreak revenge on Sienna's father?'

'OK, fair point,' said Sienna, smiling back at her. 'The dog seemed to like you though, didn't it? When did you suddenly turn into a dog whisperer?'

Sophie laughed. 'I don't know about dog whisperer,' she said. 'When he first appeared, I thought I was going to be his lunch.'

When they reached the station concourse, they were in luck. There was a train leaving in seven minutes that would reach London Waterloo just before two-thirty. Sophie looked at her watch.

'That should give us enough time to check out the museum and still get back to Abbeville House before Bunny.'

As the train snaked its way up to London, a sense of foreboding still nagged away at Sophie. Despite her joy at being back in Sienna's company, she was twitchy and agitated, and she couldn't shake off the idea that they were being followed. Every time a stranger walked through their compartment, Sophie eyed them with great suspicion. She clung to the backpack as if her life depended on it, conscious that it contained the relic Albert had entrusted to her.

On arriving at London Waterloo, they jumped onto an underground train and headed across the city towards Bloomsbury. When they emerged above ground again, the area around the British Museum was swarming with sightseers. Some were sitting quietly, enjoying the lovely spring sunshine. Others were chattering excitedly, many of them in languages Sophie didn't understand. It was a vibrant, bustling atmosphere, a hive of activity in the heart of tourist London.

'Wow, that's impressive,' said Sienna, looking up at the massive stone columns that adorned the front of the museum. 'It looks a bit like the Senate building in Galacdros. Are you sure this is just a museum?'

'Yes, it's amazing, isn't it?' said Sophie. 'My mum and dad used to take me here when I was younger. It always felt like I was walking into a royal palace.'

They made their way past the huge stone pillars and through the magnificent front door into the lobby.

'Right, we need to find the area dealing with American history,' said Sophie. 'Let's see if there's a floor plan.'

She found a visitors' guide, unfolded the map, and held it out in front of them. It took them a minute to work out how to read it, and they were so preoccupied they didn't notice what was going on around them. If they had, they would have seen a tall man with a scar on the side of his head leaving through the front door and heading back to Waterloo station.

'Ah! Room 27, Central America,' said Sophie, pointing at the map. 'Let's start there and see what we can find.'

The interior of the museum was just as impressive as the frontage, with beautifully carved ceilings and elegant marble staircases. The building had a grandeur that made the girls feel as if they were in a place of great importance. It contained some of the most significant archaeological finds of the last two centuries and was an impressive record of human history, art and culture.

'I hope whatever Mr Adamson saw is still here,' said

Sophie, as they headed through the throng of tourists. 'They probably have to change the exhibits from time to time to keep things interesting for their regular visitors.'

Room 27 was less of a room and more of a large gallery. It had a vaulted ceiling and deep red walls and was filled with countless artefacts from the ancient civilisations of Central America, including the Aztecs and the Mayans. There was so much to look at. It was difficult to take it all in.

They searched through every exhibit, painstakingly studying the labels and descriptions, hoping to find something about T.J. Stapleton. If Central American history was his specialist subject, surely there would be something about him in here. But they couldn't find a trace of him anywhere.

As the afternoon wore on, Sophie was beginning to give up hope. Then they suddenly found themselves in front of a large glass case containing a selection of treasures from a Mayan tomb. Sophie knew immediately that this was the exhibit they were looking for. She gasped and stared at it, wide-eyed with excitement.

The relics were arranged on small plinths, with a detailed description on a label at the side. And in the centre of the case was a framed black-and-white photograph that had been taken at the tomb entrance. They looked at the inscription displayed underneath. It read, "Herbert Hawkins with his two assistants and Carlos the native guide."

Sophie could feel her heart pounding away in her chest. At last, they were going to discover the true identity of T.J. Stapleton. But when she looked at the photograph more intently, she was astonished to discover that one of the young archaeologists was a woman.

For a few seconds, Sophie gazed at the photograph, trying to take it all in. She could see at once that the young man outside the tomb was a very youthful-looking Albert, but to discover that Stapleton was actually a woman was the last thing she had been expecting. Why had they assumed that she was a man? Well, largely because Bunny had given them that impression when she sent them to the address in Winchester.

Then Sophie looked at the photo once again, and a growing awareness gave her an even bigger shock.

'That's Bunny,' she said, staring at the photo open-mouthed.

'Are you sure?' said Sienna.

'Positive. I've known her all my life, and that woman in the photograph is definitely Bunny.'

'Then why did she send us on a wild goose chase all the way to Winchester?'

'I don't know,' said Sophie. She felt as if her world had been turned upside down.

'Maybe it's because she thinks Silver will return to the house, and she doesn't want you to be there when that happens,' said Sienna. 'Your parents left you in her care, so you can't blame her for wanting to get you as far away from the house as possible.'

Sophie was completely distraught.

'And now we're stuck up here in London,' she said, 'and if Bunny gets back before us she'll be alone in Abbeville House. We have to get back there. She's an elderly lady. We can't leave her to face Silver on her own.'

They burst out of Room 27, hurtled back through the museum, and sprinted down to Russell Square underground station. When they finally emerged above ground at Waterloo, the train times weren't so kind to them this time. The next service didn't leave for twenty-seven minutes. By the time they reached Abbeville House, it would be almost six-thirty in the evening.

Sophie took out her phone and tried to contact Bunny, hoping she could persuade her to drive into the town and sit somewhere safe until the girls had returned. But the call just went to voicemail.

'Bunny, it's Sophie,' she barked into the phone. 'We're on our way home. Phone me before you go back to the house. I need to talk to you urgently.' It was the only thing she could do, but it did nothing to relieve her anxiety.

While they waited on the station concourse, the idea that they were being followed continued to haunt Sophie. At one point, when she turned to talk to Sienna, she had the feeling that someone was watching her from inside the ticket office. By now, she had become so agitated she almost went over to confront the person.

'What's the matter?' Sienna asked. 'You've been in a really weird mood all day.'

'Nothing, I'm fine,' Sophie snapped. 'I just want to get back to Abbeville House.'

Sienna wasn't convinced. She had been in a lot of difficult situations with Sophie in the time they had known each other, and she had never seen her in such an irritable frame of mind.

When they finally got onto the train, Sophie's mood

didn't improve at all. She was cranky and impatient, and Sienna was determined to find out what the problem was.

'What is the matter with you?' she asked. 'Ever since we left the house this morning, you've been prickly and on edge. It's not like you, Sophie. What's going on?'

'I don't know,' Sophie answered, reluctantly accepting that Sienna might be right. 'All day I've had the feeling that we're being followed, and the slightest little thing has been setting me off. And I have this strange sense of foreboding, like something awful is about to happen.'

Sienna looked at the backpack that was sitting on Sophie's lap.

'Maybe it's that thing in your backpack,' she said. 'Bunny thinks it has bad energy. In fact, she wouldn't even let Albert keep it in the house.'

'But how could a little thing like that affect my mood?'

'I don't know,' Sienna answered. She looked up at the luggage rack above their heads. 'Why don't you put it up there for a while, so we can see whether it makes you feel any better?'

Sophie wasn't at all keen on letting go of the relic.

Someone had tried to kill Albert for it, and she had promised him she would keep it safe. But there was something odd going on, and Sienna's suggestion was worth a try. She lifted the backpack onto the luggage rack, then sat down and tried to phone Bunny again. But the voicemail message started almost immediately.

As the journey progressed, Sophie's mood began to lighten a little. They both noticed it. They even shared a joke about Sophie's fear of dogs and her friendship with Mr Adamson's dog, Aslan. Sienna was relieved to see Sophie laughing again. When they reached their destination, they decided it was probably safer if they took turns to carry the backpack. Whatever strange power the relic had, it was important that one of them wasn't carrying it around for too long.

Once they were outside the station, Sophie took out her phone and tried to contact Bunny again. To her frustration, she got the same result as last time. This was all becoming quite alarming. Why had Bunny kept her voicemail turned on all day? Surely she must have noticed all the missed calls from Sophie. And why hadn't she phoned her back? They jumped onto a bus and headed out towards Abbeville House, increasingly concerned about what they were likely to find.

It was getting dark as they walked up the gravel drive towards the house. In the twilight, everything looked sinister and eerie. There were no lights on, but one of the downstairs windows was open. It all seemed a bit odd. Sophie knocked at the door. There was no response. She knocked again, a little more firmly. To her surprise, the door swung open quite easily. Either Bunny had left in a hurry and didn't get the chance to lock up, or there was something very strange going on.

Chapter 14

Sophie pushed the door open and felt around for the light, but when she flipped the switch, they were still in darkness. The same thing happened when she tried the light in the sitting room and the tall floor lamp that stood between the two sofas.

'That's weird,' she said. 'I wonder if there's been a power cut.'

As they moved around in the half-light, the memory of Albert lying on the floor of the museum suddenly flashed into her mind. The image was so vivid and alarming that she froze for a moment, terrified that Bunny could have met the same fate.

'Bunny, are you here?' she shouted, a note of desperation in her voice. 'It's Sophie. I'm with Sienna.'

They listened for a few seconds, but there was no response.

'Something's not right here,' said Sienna.

'Yes,' Sophie answered. 'I've got a bad feeling about this. And this time I don't think it's because I'm carrying the relic.'

She took out her phone and shone the flashlight down the hallway, hoping they weren't too late and praying that Bunny was still OK. Suddenly a thick arm wrapped itself around her neck and squeezed her so tightly that she could barely breathe. There was a large presence behind her that almost lifted her off the ground. She grabbed at the arm and tried to scream out, but she could only let out a low strangulated sound.

'Shut up or I'll break your neck!' a man shouted, squeezing his arm even tighter.

He pushed her hard into the darkness, and she clattered into Sienna, knocking them both to the floor. By the time they gathered themselves, the lights had come on, and Silver was standing a few paces away, holding a gun. His monstrous size and his wild, staring eyes made Sophie recoil in horror.

'Throw the backpack over here!' he shouted.

Sophie was so frozen with fear that she couldn't move. When he shouted at her again, Sienna grabbed the backpack and threw it over to his feet. He picked it up and tipped the contents out onto the floor. Then he went through all the pockets but found nothing.

'Where is it?' he shouted.

'Where's what?' said Sophie. 'I don't know what you mean.'

'The relic!' he barked. 'I know you have it. I heard you talking about it when you first came in. Now tell me where it is, or you can say goodbye to your friend.'

He pointed the gun at Sienna's head. Sophie knew she didn't have any choice. Despite her promise not to let the relic fall into the wrong hands, she was sure he would follow through on his threat.

'The backpack has a false bottom,' she said. 'It's in a pocket under the flap.'

Silver searched the backpack once again, and this time he found what he was looking for. He took the silk cloth out of the little metal box and slowly unfolded it to reveal the prize he had been searching for. A smile spread across his cruel features.

'Excellent,' he said, staring at the relic. There was a look of wild excitement in his eyes. He appeared to be mesmerised by its power. He threw the backpack onto the floor and put the relic into his jacket pocket.

'Now, where's Stapleton?' he said.

'Who?' Sophie answered.

'Don't mess with me, girl!' Silver shouted, pointing the gun at them menacingly. 'You know who I'm talking about. Now, where is she?'

Sophie was devastated to discover that Silver knew the true identity of T.J. Stapleton. They had lost the one advantage they had over him.

'We don't know where she is,' said Sienna. 'We've been trying to contact her all afternoon, but she hasn't been answering her phone. That's why we came back here.'

Silver looked at them for a few seconds. They could sense the cogs turning in his head as he tried to work out whether he should believe them. Eventually, he seemed to make up his mind.

'OK, on your feet!' he barked.

As the girls stood up, Sienna kept her eyes firmly fixed on Silver. If he lost concentration, she might get the chance to launch an attack. He was a big man and a ruthless killer, but she was confident she could take him if the opportunity presented itself. He kept a safe distance between them, though, and Sienna knew she would have to bide her time.

'I've been doing a bit of research on you,' said Silver,

looking at Sienna disdainfully. 'You're the girl who returned The Orb to Galacdros, aren't you? You're something of a hero to the Galacdrian people. What a shame it would be if anything happened to you.'

'You don't frighten me,' said Sienna. 'The Elite know that you're hiding out in this world, and soon you'll be back in The Stockade where you belong.'

Silver laughed. It was an icy laugh. It came from somewhere that had never known warmth or affection.

'Up the stairs,' he said. 'I'll deal with The Elite and your father once the old lady has given me what I want.'

Sophie was horrified by the thought of Bunny walking into Silver's trap. She was still quite active for a woman of her age, but she would be no match for the brutality of Silver. Somehow they had to find a way to warn her.

When they reached the next floor, the hatch to the attic was open, and the ladder was already down.

'Keep walking,' Silver ordered, pointing the gun towards the ladder.

The girls continued to climb. At the top of the steps, they found themselves in a large cluttered space under the eaves of the house. Silver followed close behind, and stood half-way up the ladder with only his torso visible.

'Right,' he barked. 'I'm going downstairs to wait for Stapleton. If you make any noise or try to warn her, I'll kill her on sight. And then I'll come up here for you two. So just shut up and keep quiet.'

He started back down the steps, but stopped and poked his head back up through the hatch.

'Put your phones on the floor, and back away to the far side,' he ordered.

The girls reluctantly gave up their phones. Then Silver locked the hatch from the outside and made his way back down to the ground floor. A few seconds later the lights went out. The house had returned to darkness.

'So what do we do now?' said Sophie.

'Try to find a way out,' said Sienna defiantly. 'There's only one of him, and even though he has a gun, I'm sure we could take him if we got the chance. But first, we have to get out of here.'

'But he said he would kill Bunny if we try to warn her.'

'That was just talk. He has to keep Bunny alive for the time being. She's probably the only person who knows where the third relic is.'

Sophie reached out her hand and tried to get a sense of what was around her. She had been in this attic many times over the years, but always with the light on. In the darkness, she was just as much of a stranger here as Sienna.

'I thought he was going to forget about the phones,' she said.

'Yes, I know,' said Sienna. 'That flashlight would have been really useful right now.'

'You don't think Bunny could have hidden the last relic up here, do you? If we could find it and get out somehow, there's still a chance we could stop him.'

'I'd be surprised if she kept it up here,' Sienna answered. 'I think she'd want it to be as far away from the house as possible.'

All the time they were talking, Sienna was feeling her way around in the darkness, hoping to find something that would help them escape. It was pitch-black, and at every step, she kept stumbling into mysterious objects. But after a while, her eyes became accustomed to the darkness, and she could navigate a little more easily.

Then the clouds cleared, and moonlight streaked through a small skylight window at the far end of the attic. It dimmed for a moment before returning, brighter and more powerful this time. At last, they could make out shapes in the space around them.

Sienna dodged her way through the collection of knick-knacks and old furniture, making her way towards the skylight. It was quite a decent size, and in the silvery moonlight, it was easy to locate the latch and push the skylight window open.

'I think we've found our way out,' she said.

Sophie gasped, alarmed by what she was suggesting.

'Onto the roof? You must be joking, Sienna.'

It was a risky move, and Sienna had no desire to put her friend in danger. But she knew it was the only way they were going to get out of there.

'I know this is the last thing on earth you want to do,' she said, 'but sooner or later, Bunny is going to come back and walk right into Silver's trap. And once he's got his hands on that relic, he'll kill her on the spot, and then he'll come up here for us. We don't have any choice, Sophie. We have to go for it. We have to find a way to stop him.'

Chapter 15

Sienna hoisted herself up through the skylight and scrambled out onto the roof. The moonlight that had been her friend earlier now made her feel horribly exposed.

'I'll scout around for a while to see if I can find a way down,' she whispered. 'There's got to be a way to do it without alerting Silver.'

'Be careful,' said Sophie, reaching out to touch her arm. 'Remember, it's a long way down.'

'Don't worry,' Sienna whispered. 'I'll be back before you know it.'

Sophie smiled back at her. Then she watched as Sienna scaled up to the ridge of the roof and disappeared over to the other side.

Alone in the attic, Sophie was left to deal with the thoughts that were nagging away inside her head. Where was Bunny? She should have been back by now. And where was the third relic that Silver was so desperate to find?

She made her way over to the trapdoor that led down to the landing, listening for any sounds from down below. Everything was quiet. It tortured her to think that Silver was still lurking down there, waiting to ambush Bunny on her return. Sienna was right. They had to do something.

Up above her, she could hear Sienna's footsteps clambering around on the roof. Every now and again she would pause briefly, then shuffle along a little further. Finally, after being outside for several minutes, she crossed over to the skylight window and poked her head into the attic.

'There's a fat downpipe at the other end of the house that looks like it could hold our weight,' she whispered. 'We should be alright as long as Silver doesn't come outside or hear us moving about.'

Sophie felt a cold sweat envelop her at the thought of having to scale down the side of the house. Even though she was desperate to warn Bunny about Silver, a part of her had been hoping Sienna wouldn't find a route to the ground. Climbing down the pipe sounded like madness.

One slip and they could plummet to their deaths. But she was sure Sienna would go through with this, no matter how perilous it was. Bunny's life was in danger, and Sophie knew she would have to swallow down her fear.

'Give me your hand, and I'll help you climb out,' Sienna whispered.

She reached down and helped Sophie through the skylight, but on reaching the roof, Sophie froze for several seconds, too frightened to move. The cold, grey slate was sleek and even. There was nothing to brace her feet against and nothing to hold on to. She leaned back against the roof and tried not to think about how far it was to the ground.

'Are you OK?' Sienna asked when she saw how terrified Sophie was.

'We're a lot higher than I thought we'd be,' Sophie answered. 'I'll need a minute before we go any further.'

'Try not to look down,' said Sienna softly. 'If you look into the distance, it will help you forget how high up we are.'

The clouds had drifted away, and the moon was throwing out its silvery light, bathing the land all around them in an eerie glow. From her position up on the roof,

Sophie could see right across the extensive gardens of Abbeville House: the maze, the ruins of the old manor house, and the wooded area now shrouded in darkness. She took a few deep breaths and tried to compose herself.

'The pipe is down at the other end,' said Sienna. 'If we climb up to the ridge first, it will be safer than going straight across the tiles.' She waited for a moment, aware that Sophie was finding this challenging. 'OK, are you ready?'

Sophie nodded, then moved painfully slowly as they inched their way up towards the ridge of the roof. The tiles felt as if they had been freshly polished, and it was hard to get any type of decent grip. It was like walking up a sheet of ice.

Despite the difficult surface, they were making steady progress. But just as they were reaching the top, Sophie's foot slipped, and in a moment of panic, she made a frantic grab at Sienna's jacket. If Sienna hadn't been so well balanced, the jolt of it might have caused them both to lose their footing, sending them careering down the roof to the concrete path below.

As they desperately scrambled to steady themselves, Sophie's foot slipped again. This time one of the tiles became dislodged and started scuttling down towards the edge of the roof. In the stillness of the evening, the sound of it crashing against the concrete path was bound to alert Silver. And if he saw the shattered tile, he would know immediately where it had come from. They held their breath as the tile hurtled towards the edge of the roof, then clattered against the guttering and stopped abruptly, nestling in the gutter. It was such a narrow escape. They couldn't believe their luck.

Driven forward by the adrenaline that was now pumping through her veins, Sophie scrabbled up the tiles and clung to the ridge of the roof. She closed her eyes and took several deep breaths, trying to calm the terror that was overwhelming her. But when she opened her eyes again, she was still in the middle of a nightmare.

'Are you alright?' Sienna whispered.

Sophie nodded and swallowed hard. She was committed now, and there was no option but to get on with it. They shuffled over to the other end of the house and made their way down to where Sienna had found the downpipe. As soon as Sophie saw the pipe, her body clenched and her eyes widened with alarm. It was a sheer drop to the concrete down below. She wasn't even sure how they were going to get onto the pipe to begin with.

'OK,' Sienna whispered. 'I think it's probably best if you go first.'

Sophie inhaled sharply.

'What?' she said, staring back at her in horror. 'I can't Sienna. I wouldn't even know where to start.'

'Of course you can. Look, it will be much easier if you go first. You can hold on to me until you're safely on the pipe.'

Sophie shrank back from the edge of the roof. The challenge they faced looked almost impossible. She could barely stop herself from sliding off the roof as it was.

'I'm not sure I can do this, Sienna,' she whispered. 'We're too high up.'

'Try not to think about how high up you are. Just focus on getting onto the pipe. Once you're there, we'll worry about how to deal with the rest of it.'

It was a terrifying prospect, but Sophie realised they had to keep pressing forward. They couldn't go back to the attic. If Sienna was right about Silver, then sitting and waiting for him to return would mean certain death. Their only option was to get away from the house and find a way to warn Bunny. Sophie took a deep breath and nodded.

'OK,' said Sienna in a low voice. 'I'll brace my feet against the gutter and hold on to one of your hands while you climb onto the pipe. Try to get your feet onto one of the brackets that hold the pipe to the wall. It should be about three feet down. Once you're there, we'll decide what to do next.'

'And how are you going to get down with no one to hold on to?'

'Don't worry about me,' said Sienna. 'Just focus on getting to that first bracket. And whatever you do, don't look down.'

With her heart pounding in her chest, Sophie inched her way over the edge of the roof. She clung to Sienna with her right hand, while her left hand gripped the guttering and her feet groped around for the pipe. It felt like she was dangling over the edge of a cliff. Scraping her feet against the pipe and the walls, she searched around for the bracket. But she couldn't find it anywhere. Surely her feet should have reached it by now. How far down was it? Had she missed it altogether? She started to panic, and she was about to tell Sienna to pull her back up, when her foot finally found something solid to rest on. As relief surged through her, she paused and took a few deep breaths.

'Right,' she said, exhaling slowly. 'My feet are on the bracket.'

'Good,' Sienna whispered. 'I've got a firm grip on you, so you can let go of the gutter and grab the pipe with your left hand.'

For a few seconds, Sophie couldn't bring herself to let go of the gutter. But clinging to Sienna with her right hand, she eventually moved her other hand down and grabbed hold of the pipe. Soon she was holding on to the pipe with both hands.

'That's great,' said Sienna. 'Now try to take all the weight on your hands, and slide your feet down to the next bracket. It should be about another three feet. And don't look down. Just feel for it with your foot.'

But when Sophie lifted one of her feet away from the wall, her body began to shake uncontrollably. The space below her felt like a vast chasm, and she couldn't bring herself to move her other foot. She clung to the pipe, consumed with fear and terrified she was about to plummet to the ground.

'I can't do this, Sienna,' she said. 'It's too much. I won't be able to hold my weight. Pull me up! I don't want to stay here. Please, Sienna, pull me back up!'

Chapter 16

Sienna leaned over the edge of the roof and grabbed Sophie's arm. She could see that her friend was terrified, but now that she was on the pipe, it would be too dangerous to attempt to pull her back up. One slip and they could both go crashing to the ground. They had to keep going. There was no alternative. She held on to Sophie with a firm grip and tried to offer some reassurance.

'It's OK,' she said. 'You're doing great. Just stay where you are, and we'll work out what to do next.'

Sophie felt totally numb. She stared straight ahead, clinging on with both hands.

'I can't take my feet off the pipe,' she said. 'I'll fall. I know I will.'

'No, you won't,' said Sienna. 'You're a lot stronger than you think. Why don't you move your hands down a bit? Then you can grip the pipe with your legs and slide down it a little at a time.'

Sophie bit her lip and moved one of her hands a little further down the pipe. Once she had a firm grip, she slid the other hand down. But her feet still felt like lead, and she couldn't bring herself to lift them off the bracket.

'I'm sorry, Sophie,' Sienna whispered, 'but we have to keep going. Bunny could be back at any minute, and she's going to need our help.'

Sophie clung to the pipe, trembling with fear, but she had to admit that Sienna was right. With great reluctance, she gripped the pipe with her knees and began to slowly slide down towards the next bracket. Up above, Sienna was watching her very carefully.

'That's good,' said Sienna in a hushed tone. 'There's no rush. Just take it at your own pace.'

In the silent tension, Sophie scrabbled her feet around for any kind of foothold. For a moment, she thought she was going to black out. Then she noticed she had been holding her breath for far too long. She paused, inhaled and exhaled slowly, and carried on down the pipe. Soon she had made it to the next bracket, and she could see Sienna up above her, climbing off the edge of the roof onto the pipe.

As she struggled to cope with one of the most terrifying experiences of her life, Sophie was astonished at how simple Sienna made the process look. With relative ease, she was soon just a few feet above Sophie, urging her to keep going.

For a while, they appeared to be making progress. Sophie even believed she might be able to do this. Then the pipe made a creaking and groaning sound, and to Sophie's horror, the bracket above her suddenly jerked away from the wall. She let out an involuntary yelp and was thrown into a panic, terrified that she had alerted Silver to their presence.

'Keep going,' Sienna whispered. 'It might not hold us for much longer.'

No sooner had she finished speaking, than a door at the back of the house swung open, and the hulking frame of Silver emerged into the garden. He shone a flashlight into the bushes that surrounded the house, searching for the source of the noise.

'Who's there?' he shouted, pointing a gun into the darkness.

The girls kept perfectly still. The pipe appeared to be holding, but for how much longer? Surely it was only a matter of time before they came crashing to the ground.

And if the fall didn't kill them, Silver certainly would.

Down below, they could see Silver prowling around the garden, flicking the flashlight into every conceivable hiding place. They were completely exposed. If he looked up, he would definitely see them. They were only twenty feet above his head, clinging to an unstable pipe, and there was nothing they could do to escape or hide.

A rustling sound came from the bushes a little further along the path. When Silver spun around and flashed the light in its direction, a pair of glowing animal eyes stared back at him defiantly. This was their domain, and they were curious to know who this intruder was. He moved slowly towards the eyes, pointing the gun at the bushes.

In a sudden burst of action, a small furry creature flashed across in front of him and disappeared off into the night. It seemed to take Silver by surprise. He stood and watched as it melted into the shadows, and after an agonising wait, he switched the flashlight off and went back inside the house.

Sophie closed her eyes and exhaled with relief. But just as she did, the bracket gave way and the top of the pipe jerked sharply away from the wall. The jolt of it was such a shock that it almost caused her to lose her grip.

She clung on for dear life, desperately hoping that the rest of the brackets would hold.

It was time for drastic action and Sienna knew it. Even though she was a few feet higher than Sophie, she pushed herself away from the wall and dropped down onto the path, crashing to the ground and rolling over onto the grassy border that surrounded the house.

For a few seconds, there was a terrifying silence. They knew the noise of Sienna's crash-landing could have alerted Silver, and he might burst into the garden at any minute. To make matters worse, the pipe above Sophie looked like it was about to collapse. Shinning down the pipe as quickly as she dared, Sophie dropped the last few feet onto the path and held her breath. Her legs were trembling from the exertion of the climb, and her heart was pounding in her chest.

The door at the back of the house was slightly ajar. It was impossible to make out any shapes in the pitch-black interior, but she knew Silver could be just a few feet away, watching her and hoping she would lead him to Sienna. He never appeared, though, and the girls didn't wait around long enough to give him a second chance.

Clouds had moved in to blot out the moon, and in

the dim light, they crept away from the house towards the well-manicured hedges that formed the edge of the interior garden. There was no sign of Bunny's car at the front of the house. Sophie was relieved to know that the girls weren't too late.

'Do you think Silver knows there's a skylight in the attic?' she asked, as they waited in the darkness.

'Maybe.' said Sienna. 'But as we're girls, he probably thought we'd be too frightened to climb out onto the roof and scale down the side of the house.'

Sophie smiled. 'Yeah, only an idiot would do something as reckless as that.'

'Or someone who is living their life as a tiger,' said Sienna, smiling back at her.

The house was still in darkness, and Sienna knew it could be hours before Bunny returned. She scoured the surrounding area, trying to decide what their next move should be.

'So where do you think the third relic is?' she asked.

'I don't know,' said Sophie. 'I'd be surprised if it was in the house, though, particularly after what Bunny said about it.'

'What about the museum?'

'It's possible, but a lot of the exhibits were destroyed

in the fire. If it was in there, it could be lost forever.'

'So where else is there? How big is this estate? Is there anywhere else she could have hidden it?'

'Well,' said Sophie. 'The garden stretches back quite a way from the house. There's the woodland area that you can just make out over there, and at the other side of the path there's the herb garden and a maze.'

'A maze?' said Sienna. 'That sounds promising. How big is it?'

'It's fairly big and covers quite a large area of the garden. The hedges are usually about twelve feet tall, but at the moment they're overgrown and in need of a trim. It's easy to get completely lost in there.'

'OK, that's definitely worth a look. What else is there?'

'The ruins of the old manor house are at the far side of the gardens. The house dates back to the fifteenth century, and in its day it was quite impressive. Only the walls are still standing, though. We used to picnic up there when I was younger, but I never liked going inside. It always gave me the creeps.'

As Sophie finished saying the words, the girls looked at one another in silent recognition. It was obvious they were both thinking the same thing. Maybe the ruins affected Sophie's mood in the same way that carrying the backpack had earlier today. And perhaps that was because every time she visited the ruins, she was close to the other relic.

'We need to get to the ruins of that old house,' said Sienna. 'We need to get there right now.'

Chapter 17

The last of the clouds were drifting away to the east, and once again they had the moon to light their way. They skirted past the outside of the maze, made their way across the overgrown gardens, and headed for the dilapidated ruins of the old manor house.

The site was a few hundred metres away, on the crest of a slope that led down to the lake. The roof of the building had long since gone, but what remained of the walls still stood there defiantly, stubbornly resisting the ravages of the weather and time. Sophie had never been there at night before. In the moonlight, the house looked spectral and ghostly — a shell of the magnificent dwelling it had once been.

'So where do we start?' said Sophie once they had reached the site.

'Well, it could be anywhere,' said Sienna. 'Let's walk

around for a while and see if any particular spot affects your mood.'

They moved around the site for several minutes. The ground inside the house was a tangle of wild plants and weeds, as nature fought to reclaim what had once been hers. There was no sign of disrupted soil or evidence that anything might be buried there. And at no point did Sophie feel discernibly different.

'This is weird,' she said. 'I'm not picking up anything at all. You don't think Bunny could have moved it, do you?'

'Maybe it takes a while for it to affect you,' said Sienna. 'Perhaps you need to shut down your rational mind and just tune into your emotions.'

'How do you mean?'

'Well, why don't you close your eyes and let me guide you around the area? Then you won't be able to make judgments based on what you can see. You can blot everything out and focus on how you are feeling.'

Sophie was sceptical that this would make any difference, but she agreed to try it, anyway. She closed her eyes, held Sienna's hand and allowed herself to be guided around the site. It was slow going. Despite her trust in Sienna, she felt uncomfortable not being in control, and it wasn't long before she wanted to give up. The longer they searched, the more doubtful she became. They had given it a try, and she was now convinced that the relic wasn't there. When she banged her toe into a rock that was sticking up out of the tightly packed earth, she had finally had enough.

'OK, that's it!' she shouted. 'Why didn't you tell me there was a rock sticking up? I trusted you. You were supposed to be looking out for me.'

It was totally out of character, and Sienna knew it.

'I think we've found the spot,' she said.

'What?' Sophie barked. 'What are you talking about?'

'Listen to yourself, Sophie. This isn't like you at all. Something has got under your skin and is making you behave aggressively.'

Despite her bad temper, Sophie knew immediately that Sienna was right, and there was a good chance that the relic was close by. Maybe the rock was there to mark the spot where it was buried. Sienna knelt down and scratched at the earth around the rock, using the sharp end of a thick branch, but she barely managed to scrape the surface soil away.

'If the relic is under this rock,' she said, 'how are we going to get it out? It'll take ages to dig it up with this.'

'Bunny usually keeps some tools in the shed next to

the herb garden,' said Sophie. 'Let's go over there and take a look.'

They rushed back through the thick grass, aware that time wasn't on their side. In the distance, they could see the outline of Abbeville House. There was no sign of Bunny's car, and the house was still in total darkness. It was a welcome sight. If they were quick, there was still a chance they could dig up the relic and get back to the house in time to warn Bunny.

Before too long, they were standing outside a small shed at the edge of a well-kept herb garden.

'Oh no, it's locked,' said Sophie.

Sienna had no intention of letting that stand in their way.

'Sorry about this, Bunny,' she said, picking up a large rock and smashing it into the padlock. At first, it didn't make much of an impression, but three more heavy strikes and the lock was lying on the ground.

It was pitch black inside the shed. They groped around for a while, searching by touch, and eventually found some old gardening tools, including a spade and a small trowel.

'These will do,' said Sophie. 'Let's hope it isn't buried too far down.'

By the time they got back to the ruins of the old manor house, the moon was high in the sky, and the night air had become crisp and cold. They looked back towards Abbeville House. It was still in darkness, and there was no sign of life. But as Sienna smashed the spade into the soil and started digging at the earth around the rock, a light appeared at the far end of the driveway. A pair of headlights swung through the gates and headed up the gravel towards the house. It was Bunny's car. She had finally arrived back from the hospital, and the girls knew what horrors were awaiting her.

'So what do we do now?' Sophie asked. 'We can't leave Bunny to deal with this on her own. She's an elderly lady. She needs our help.'

'I know,' said Sienna, 'but in the time it will take us to get back to the house, Bunny will have already arrived and been confronted by Silver.'

The car pulled up outside the house. They could see the faint outline of Bunny as she walked across the gravel towards the door. A few seconds after she entered the house, the lights came on. The girls knew exactly what she was now going through.

'We have to do something,' said Sophie.

'I'm sorry, Sophie,' said Sienna. 'I think we should dig up the relic first.'

'But we can't leave Bunny to face Silver on her own.'

'I'm afraid we have to. Think about it. Silver needs to keep Bunny alive for the time being. She's the only person who can lead him to that last relic. But if we can get our hands on it first, and hide it away somewhere, there's still a chance we can stop him and rescue Bunny.'

Sophie stared across the gardens towards Abbeville House, imagining the horrific ordeal that Bunny was now going through. It was heartbreaking to have to leave her to her fate, but Sienna was right. They had to get to the last relic before Silver. There was no time to deliberate or delay.

Sienna dug forcefully at the packed earth around the rock. Soon she had dislodged enough of it to roll the rock away, and she was powering her way through the top level of soil. When she smashed her spade into something solid, the girls looked at one another in anticipation.

'That could be it,' said Sophie, dropping to her knees beside the hole.

After scraping away the loose earth with the trowel, they pulled a small metal box out of the ground. It was identical to the box that Albert had given Sophie two days earlier, and inside, wrapped up in the same silk cloth, was the relic. It looked like an innocuous piece of gold. But Sophie and Sienna knew better than that. There was power in that little twist of gold, and Sophie was determined to stop Silver from getting his hands on it.

'We should hide it somewhere nearby,' she said. 'Then we can go back to the house and help Bunny.'

But it was too late for them to follow through on their plan. When they looked back towards the house, they saw a light flickering in the distance, and it appeared to be heading in their direction. They wouldn't have to go back to the house after all. Silver was now coming to them instead.

It was a great relief when they saw Bunny walking ahead of him, holding the flashlight. Every now and again, she pointed the flashlight at the old ruins and waved it back and forth. It pulsated like a lighthouse, warning the girls of Silver's imminent arrival.

Sienna quickly filled in the hole and rolled the large rock back into place, stamping down the earth to disguise that the soil had recently been dug up. Then they ducked into the bushes at the other side of the crumbling wall and waited. There was no time for them to do anything else. Silver and Bunny were at the crest of the slope, and they were heading across the grass towards the old manor house.

Chapter 18

In the grey-white glow of the moonlight, Silver's silhouette cut a nightmarish figure. He towered over Bunny like a monstrous troll, urging her forward while pointing a gun at her back. And he had come prepared. As they entered the ruins of the old house, Sophie could see that in his other hand he was carrying a spade.

When they arrived at the spot where the relic was buried, Bunny noticed immediately that someone had been digging there recently. There was a scattering of loose earth nearby and the faint outline of a footprint where Sienna had trodden the soil back down again. It lifted her spirits to think the girls might have beaten Silver to it.

'Is this it?' Silver grunted, looking at the rock.

'As far as I can remember,' said Bunny.

'Sit over there,' he said, pointing at a log several feet

away. 'And keep that flashlight on the spot where I'm digging.'

He put the gun in his pocket, heaved the heavy rock out of the way, and started to dig. After about a minute, there was quite a big hole, and he was becoming frustrated at not having found anything.

'How far down did you bury it?' he barked.

'Not as far down as that,' Bunny answered, a smile flickering across her features. 'If it was still there, you would have found it by now. I think someone must have got here before you.'

'Don't lie to me, old lady!' he shouted.

'Well, you can keep digging if you want, but I'm telling you that someone else got here first.'

Silver threw the spade to the ground and pulled the gun back out of his pocket.

'Who else knew it was here?' he barked, dragging her to her feet and pushing the gun against her head. 'Tell me, or I'll finish you off right here and now.'

'No one,' said Bunny defiantly. 'So I'm afraid you're going to have to work it out for yourself.'

He stared at her fixedly through narrowed eyes. If she was telling the truth, she was no longer of any use to him, so perhaps he should just kill her now. But what if she was lying? What if she knew where the relic was, after all?

Gritting his teeth in frustration, he looked into the darkness that surrounded the ruins. As far as he knew, the only other people who could have known about the relic were the old man at the museum and those two girls. But the girls were back at the house, locked in the attic. Or were they? Could they have escaped somehow? Could they have worked out where the relic was and dug it up while he was waiting for the old lady to return? If they had, they couldn't be that far away. There wouldn't have been time.

He pushed Bunny to the ground and called out to the surrounding area in a loud voice.

'OK, you little brats. You probably think you're very clever getting here before me, but I'll give you ten seconds to hand over what I'm looking for, or I'm going to put a bullet into the old lady's head. And don't think I won't do it. I've killed before, and I'm perfectly happy to do it again.'

'Don't do it, Sophie,' Bunny shouted. 'Get back to the house and call the police.'

'Shut up, old lady!' Silver barked, 'or I won't even wait for ten seconds.'

Sienna knew of Silver's reputation, and she knew he wouldn't think twice about killing Bunny and then coming after them. But if they gave him the relic, he would probably kill them all, anyway. There had to be a way to buy some time, so she could catch him off guard and try to get the better of him.

'Last chance,' Silver shouted, holding the gun against Bunny's head.

The girls looked at one another in quiet resignation. They knew they didn't have a choice.

'OK,' Sienna shouted. 'We're coming out. Don't shoot.'

Sophie could feel her legs trembling as the girls emerged from the bushes. A feeling of dread swept over her. She thought about flinging the metal box into the overgrown gardens, hoping it would be lost forever. But Silver now looked deranged enough to kill them both on the spot. When they reached the inside of the old ruins, he took a step forward and pointed the gun at Sienna.

'You!' he said. 'Stay where you are.' Then he turned to Sophie. 'And you! Bring that box over here.'

A reptilian smile spread across his face. This was the moment he had been dreaming about all those nights when he was incarcerated in a stinking prison in

Galacdros. At last, he would unite the relics and feel the power of the gods coursing through his veins. He would be immortal, and those who had opposed him would pay a very heavy price.

As she walked reluctantly towards him, Sophie realised that the situation now looked desperate. She had promised Albert she wouldn't let the relic fall into the wrong hands, yet she was about to hand Silver the final piece of the puzzle. This couldn't be allowed to happen. Despite the risk involved, she knew she would have to take drastic action.

Hooking her foot into a tangle of weeds, she stumbled forward and dropped the metal box into the darkness. As Silver raged in horror, Bunny acted on impulse. She shone the flashlight directly into his eyes, dazzling him with its glare, and as he threw up his hand to shield himself from the light, Sienna darted forward to make up the ground between them. She powered into Silver, slammed her forearm into his throat, and grabbed hold of the hand that held the gun.

The seconds that followed were frenzied and intense. As Silver and Sienna wrestled for control of the gun, Sophie scrabbled around on the ground, frantically searching for the missing relic. The earth was thick with weeds, and in the darkness, it was an almost impossible task.

Bunny was desperate to lend Sophie a hand, but she could see that Silver was gradually getting the better of Sienna. She rushed over to where they were struggling for control of the gun and smashed the heavy flashlight into the side of Silver's head. He lashed out with his foot, knocking her backwards onto the ground.

The battle for the gun was ferocious. Silver was bigger and more powerful than Sienna, but she fought with a tenacity he had never encountered before. Each of them had two hands on the gun, and they both knew that a momentary lack of concentration could be fatal.

When they crashed against the crumbling wall, Sienna stumbled awkwardly, and for a moment Silver was in control of the gun. This was the opening he had been fighting for. He twisted the gun and pointed it directly at Sienna's head. Then he pulled the trigger. But as he did, Bunny smashed him hard on the side of the head with the discarded spade, knocking him off balance and causing him to misdirect his aim. The bullet whistled past Sienna's head, taking a small piece out of her ear.

Before Silver could recover, Bunny smashed him

again with the spade. He reeled backwards, and as he turned to point the gun at Bunny, Sienna launched another brutal attack. She slammed into him with a series of savage blows, knocking him back on his heels and sending him tumbling through the gap in the wall where the window had once been. Overwhelmed by Sienna's onslaught, he crashed to the ground at the other side and rolled down the incline towards the lake.

'I've got it,' Sophie shouted, holding up the metal box and the relic. 'Come on, let's get out of here.'

They ran through the overgrown grass, desperate to put some distance between themselves and Silver, but they could only move as fast as Bunny could run. When they reached the herb garden, Sophie turned and looked back towards the old ruins. She could see the ragged and bloodied figure of Silver standing outside the old manor house. He shouted angry threats and fired a couple of shots in their direction. But good fortune was on their side. The bullets missed their target and zipped away into the night.

'We won't be able to outrun him,' said Sienna. 'We have to find somewhere to hide.'

'Head for the maze,' said Bunny. 'He'll never find us in there.'

They fled across the garden towards the tall hedges that loomed up out of the darkness. It had been a long time since Bunny had moved so quickly, and the exertion of the run left her breathless. When they finally entered the maze, she was gasping and wheezing, and she had to lean on Sophie while she recovered.

'Who is this man?' Bunny asked in between breaths.

'His name is Silver,' said Sienna, 'and we think he's the man who attacked Albert.'

It wasn't long before they heard footsteps prowling around outside. If he had been a more patient man, Silver would never have been enticed into the maze. He would have concealed himself outside and waited for Bunny and the girls to emerge. But Silver's confidence was also his biggest weakness. He believed that if anyone could find a way out of this labyrinth, it was him. It held no fear for someone of his self-proclaimed genius.

Inside the puzzle of hedges, Bunny led them towards the inner part of the maze. She had been in there many times and believed she knew these channels better than anyone. But in the pitch-black of the evening, she found it hard to navigate. The layout didn't feel the same. It was dark and unfamiliar, and having taken a few wrong turns, she realised they were heading for a dead-end.

Finally, after doubling back, they reached a spot where she was confident they wouldn't be discovered.

'Let's wait here for a moment,' she whispered. 'Once we're sure he's inside, we can circle around to the exit and leave him stranded.'

They stood in silence for a few minutes, hoping that Silver would take the bait. Soon they could hear jagged breathing and heavy footsteps, and they knew he had followed them into the maze. They listened to him tramping around amongst the hedges. He seemed to be getting closer.

Something rattled a branch at the other side of the maze, and Silver fired several shots towards the noise. In the silence that followed, Sophie hoped that an innocent, nocturnal animal hadn't just paid the ultimate price for being inquisitive.

'I know you're in here,' Silver shouted, 'and you won't be able to hide from me forever. Now that I know who you are, I will hunt you down for the rest of your lives. And the longer you make me wait for what is mine, the more hideous and painful your deaths will be.'

Bunny and the girls kept perfectly still. He was only a few feet away from them, in an adjacent passage that ran parallel to theirs. But in the twisting labyrinth of tunnels, he might just as well have been several miles away.

'You know it doesn't have to be like this,' he shouted. 'You could walk away from here if you just give me what is mine. It is of no value to you. Why are you risking your lives for just a little twist of metal?'

Once again, Bunny and the girls didn't respond. The only thing that pierced the silence was the sound of Silver's tramping feet and his menacing threats.

'Give it to me!' he screamed out in anger. 'Give it to me, or I'll kill you all and feed your bodies to the rats!'

A few minutes passed. Sophie stayed rooted to the spot, fearful of every shadow. Then she suddenly became aware that she couldn't hear Silver's footsteps anymore. The only sound she could hear was the wind rustling through the nearby trees and her own shallow breathing. A cold sweat passed over her. Somewhere in the maze, a deranged killer was on their trail, and now she wasn't even sure where he was. They kept perfectly still, listening out for a clue to his whereabouts, but all they could hear was the silence.

'Where is he?' Sienna whispered. 'He was here a moment ago and now he seems to have disappeared.'

Bunny looked up and down the channel of hedges,

trying to decide on their next move. From where Silver was when they heard him a few minutes ago, there's only one direction he could have gone in. But he didn't seem to be anywhere near there now. So where was he? She leaned over towards the girls and pulled them in close.

'He's probably still in the maze, so we should try to get out and make a run for the car. With any luck, he'll be stuck somewhere near the middle, and it will take him ages to find the exit.'

The girls nodded in agreement. They were happy to let Bunny lead the way.

'And let me take that thing for a while,' Sienna whispered, reaching out to take the relic from Sophie. 'We don't want it playing any more tricks on your mind.'

It was a relief to hand over the metal box. Sophie knew the effect it could have on her, and she was terrified enough without the relic amplifying her fear any further. She handed the box to Sienna, and the three of them moved off silently through the darkness.

It was a slow process. Bunny was sure she knew the way out of the maze, but in the gloomy light, nothing seemed quite so clear cut. During the day, there were gaps that let the light through, making it easier to navigate. But the darkness had created a level playing field where she was almost as disadvantaged as Silver.

They inched their way forward, hoping they would turn a corner and everything would suddenly fall into place. But every channel they turned into looked just the same as the last — a tall passage of hedges that led off into the dark.

Sophie was becoming increasingly alarmed. She closed her eyes and tried to imagine the maze in daylight, hoping her memory could provide some inspiration. Over the years, she had been inside this maze many times, and she never had the slightest trouble finding her way back out again. But that was always during the daytime. And on those occasions, there wasn't a cold-blooded killer on her trail.

How had this happened? Hiding in the maze should have given them an advantage. They were luring Silver into a trap, and once he was inside, they would leave him there while they made their escape. Now it felt like they were the prey. And to make matters worse, they had no idea where Silver was. She began to wonder if they would ever get out alive.

Chapter 19

The silence was abruptly broken by the hoot of an owl, followed by the rhythmic beating of wings as it soared into the air. Under the cloak of darkness, it circled the maze, searching for its hapless prey. Hiding in the labyrinth of hedges, Sophie knew how those ill-fated rodents felt.

They crept down to the next corner. It was a junction of four different paths, each leading off into the dark. Bunny paused for a moment, peering down each of the passages in turn.

'I'm sorry girls,' she whispered, 'just give me a minute while I get my bearings.'

For a few moments, they waited at the junction while Bunny considered their options. To Sophie, all the passages looked exactly the same. They now seemed to be relying on luck more than judgment.

'I think it might be this one,' Bunny whispered, although she sounded a little unsure.

But before they could set off again, they heard Silver's heavy footsteps. He was somewhere close by, and he was heading in their direction. They bolted into the channel they had come from, leaned back into the overgrown hedge, and hoped they could blend into the darkness. Sophie's heart was pounding in her chest. Her mouth was dry, and she seemed to have lost the ability to swallow.

Seconds later, Silver arrived at the junction. He was only about twenty feet away from them. They listened to his mutterings while he considered which direction to take. His deliberation seemed to go on forever. When he started down the passage they were hiding in, Sophie held her breath and gripped Sienna's hand, terrified that they were about to be discovered. But he paused after a few paces and stood quite still, listening to the sounds of the night.

Something rustled the hedges in another part of the maze. On hearing it, Silver spun around and fired at the sound in anger. Then he darted away towards the noise and disappeared into one of the other passages. Sophie closed her eyes and let out a long, slow breath of relief.

How had he not noticed them? At one point, they were only a few feet away from him, yet it was almost as if they were invisible. Just like the owl, they had used the cloak of darkness. But this time, the prey had outwitted the predator.

They set off with fresh hope, buoyed by the knowledge that Silver was still inside the maze. Clouds were now covering the moon, and it was hard to make out more than a few feet in front of them. It felt like they were walking through an endless tunnel. Every step they took seemed crashingly loud to Sophie. Even their breathing sounded as if it might give their position away. Then the moon suddenly burst through a gap in the clouds, throwing light down onto the ground, and when they looked to the end of the tall row of hedges, they could see the exit.

The relief they all felt was overwhelming. Bunny looked like she couldn't have continued for much longer. They moved as quickly and quietly as they could, heading for the gap in the hedge. In a few more seconds they would be free, and, with luck, Silver would be trapped inside the giant hedgerow puzzle.

When they spilt out into the garden, the air felt cleaner and fresher, and it lifted their spirits to be able to see into the distance again. They darted back towards the house, moving as quietly as they could. The longer Silver thought they were still inside the maze, the more time they would have to make their escape. As they fled through the darkness, Sophie kept turning around to check that they weren't being followed. Every second they gained could be the difference between life and death. She wanted to run as fast as she could — put all her remaining energy into pounding across the garden towards the car. But Bunny was soon flagging, and they could only move at her faltering pace.

By the time they reached the house, Bunny was struggling to keep going. Sophie ducked inside and grabbed the car keys off the table, and soon all three of them were sitting in the car, ready to go. When they looked out through the rear window, there was still no sign of Silver. Not much longer, and they would be safe in the town where they could disappear into the bustle of the evening. But when Bunny put the key into the ignition and tried to start the engine, it groaned and spluttered noisily, and refused to spring into life.

'Come on, Matilda,' Bunny pleaded, 'please don't let me down now.'

She turned the ignition key again. The engine

continued to splutter and groan.

'What's happening, Bunny?' said Sienna. 'We've got to get going.'

Bunny tried again. The engine coughed and almost sparked into life. Then it spluttered and died once more.

'Sorry girls, I don't understand…'

They heard a loud crack, and the rear windscreen suddenly shattered, showering the inside of the car with fragments of glass. Silver was out of the maze, and he was coming in their direction. They heard another loud crack. A bullet whizzed past the car and disappeared into the night. Sienna knew they had to get out of there. And quickly.

'Back to the house!' she shouted. 'Come on, let's go!'

She pushed the car door open, and they bolted into the house. They would only have a few seconds' advantage. Sienna knew they would have to make it count. Without saying a word, she bounded up the stairs and headed for the room at the back of the house. By the time Sophie and Bunny arrived, she had already pulled back the fireplace door to reveal the secret hiding place behind it. As they squeezed into the space and pulled the door shut behind them, Silver's voice was already booming out down below.

He marauded through the house, shouting out threats and demanding that they show themselves. It sounded as if he had lost his mind. Whether the blows he had taken to the head were affecting his mental state, or carrying the relics around had taken its toll, they couldn't be sure. But there was one thing they were certain of. They needed to stay well hidden from his madness. Their lives depended on it.

It was a long wait. Sophie was afraid they could be stuck in the tiny space for hours. As she tried to stay calm, Silver prowled around the house, muttering away to himself and searching for a clue to their whereabouts. From time to time, he would pause and yell horrific threats at them. Eventually, he stopped on the landing and shouted out in frustration.

'I know you're in here somewhere, and if you don't show yourselves, I'm going to burn this house down with you inside it.'

A few minutes later, he entered the room where they were hiding, and they could hear him sloshing liquid around inside a container. Sophie could smell petrol. Silver must have found the spare can Bunny kept in the shed at the back of the house, and now he intended to use it to burn the house down. As he went from room to room, they could hear him shouting out more deranged threats.

'What are we going to do?' Bunny whispered. She sounded completely distraught.

'If he burns the house down, he'll destroy the relic,' Sienna answered. 'And he knows that. He's got to be bluffing.'

'But what if he isn't?' Sophie whispered. 'He's already set fire to the museum.'

'Unfortunately, we have no way of knowing,' said Sienna. 'But if we show ourselves, he'll take the relic and kill us all. I think our best option is to stay where we are for the time being.'

The time passed slowly. After a while, they couldn't hear Silver's threats anymore. They sat in silence, not daring to believe that it was over. Could he have given up and left the house? Or was he waiting in the shadows, like the cunning predator that he was? In the confines of their hiding place, a host of dreadful outcomes kept flashing into Sophie's mind. She closed her eyes and tried to still her imagination.

As the minutes ticked by, Sienna began to feel restless. She knew it would be a big mistake to come out of hiding too soon, but they couldn't stay where they were forever. At some point, they would have to take a chance and emerge from behind the fireplace. She shifted her position and leaned across to Bunny.

'What are the chances we'll be able to get the car started?' she whispered.

'Why?' said Bunny. 'Do you think he's gone?'

'I don't know. But we won't find out until we try to get away from here.'

They knew it would be a risk to leave the safety of their hiding place. If Silver was still lurking in the house, it could mean certain death. But they hadn't heard him moving around for quite a while.

'If we make it out of the house, why don't we head for the woods?' Sophie whispered. 'It's so dark in there; he'll never be able to find us. And there's a gate at the far side that leads to the main road into town.'

'Sophie's right,' Bunny whispered. 'We should head for the woods.'

Sienna inched the fireplace door open and peered out into the room. There was no sign of Silver, but the smell of petrol was intense. She pushed the door open a little further and carefully climbed out. No words were spoken as the others followed. When she looked out onto the landing, it all seemed quiet. They moved as if they were walking on very thin ice.

As they made their way down the stairs, Sienna clung to the metal box containing the relic, aware that she was fighting for her father's life just as much as she was fighting for her own. They reached the front door and stepped out onto the gravel path. There was still no sign of Silver.

Seeing the woods in the distance raised Sophie's spirits a little. Despite the threat they were facing, she knew they were only a short walk from safety. In a few more seconds, they could be moving across the garden, heading for the sanctuary of the trees.

But her optimism turned to horror, when a ghoulish figure emerged from the darkness. It was Silver, and he looked like he had stepped out of the gates of hell. His hair was matted with blood that had seeped from a large cut on the top of his head, and one of his eyes had completely closed after a heavy blow from the flashlight. In the light of the moon, the scar on his head glistened below his ragged hair. And in his blood-splattered and torn clothes, he was both nauseating and terrifying in equal measure. He looked deranged, and there was a crazed look of evil in his eyes.

Chapter 20

Nobody moved for several seconds. Sophie wanted to run, bolt from the scene in a desperate attempt to escape. But she was so rigid with fear she couldn't even bring herself to scream. It was as if her brain had shut down and was no longer sending out instructions. She stared at the horrific figure standing in front of her, convinced she was about to die. Finally, Silver raised his gun and took a few paces forward.

'You!' he shouted, looking at Sienna. 'Bring that box over here and put it on the ground.'

Holding the box that could decide her father's fate, Sienna walked towards Silver, watching him carefully as she approached. He was now so unhinged and unpredictable; she knew she had to be ready for anything. When she was only a few feet away from him, he threw up his hand.

'That's far enough,' he said. 'Put it down and get back over there with the others.'

Sienna dropped onto one knee and placed the box on the ground, studying Silver for any lapse in concentration. He wasn't that far away. If she could get a little closer, there was still a chance she could launch a sudden attack. But could she get to him before the bullet reached her? Her father's life was at stake, so it was a risk she was willing to take. Silver seemed to sense the threat, though. He took a few paces back and pointed the gun at her head.

'I said, get back over there with the others.'

Clenching her jaw in frustration, Sienna stood up and backed away to rejoin Sophie and Bunny.

'Now, sit down; all three of you.'

They huddled on the ground, aware that they were now at his mercy. Sophie could feel her body shaking uncontrollably. She thought about the stories Sienna had told her of Silver's murderous past. Of how those who opposed him had vanished — never to be seen again. Was this how it was all going to end?

'Your interference has been like a shard of glass in my foot,' said Silver, 'and for that, I intend to make you suffer. But first, you can witness my elevation to god-like status.'

He picked up the box that Sienna had placed on the ground and stared across at her menacingly.

'When your father sent me to The Stockade, he robbed me of everything I had worked for. He took away my freedom and my reason for being alive. And at my mockery of a trial, he told me I would be incarcerated forever.'

A cruel smile flickered across his ravaged features.

'It will be poetic justice when he is brought before me to watch his only daughter die.'

'And by doing that, you will show the people of Galacdros that my father was right to lock you away,' said Sienna.

Silver scoffed and shook his head with contempt.

'The people of Galacdros are a cowardly rabble,' he said. 'They would follow a sheep if you put a senator's robe on it.'

He turned to Sophie and drilled into her with his demonic eyes.

'You will go to Galacdros with a message for Memphis. Tell him if he wants to see his precious daughter again, he must travel here and bow down before me.'

'No!' Sienna shouted. 'The journey through the portal could kill her.'

'If she does not return, I will send the old lady,' said Silver. 'I'm only keeping you all alive because you are still useful to me.'

He knelt down, placed the metal box on the ground and took the other two relics from his pocket. After carefully fitting them together, he opened up the metal box and took out the third relic. It looked like he was carrying out a religious ceremony.

'The final piece of the puzzle,' he said, his eyes wide with excitement. 'When I fit the last section and create the Imperium, the power of the gods will flow through me, and I will be immortal.'

He pushed the last of the relics into position. Then, summoning the gods to commune with him, he stood up and held the Imperium aloft. Immediately, it began to pulsate and glow. Silver could feel its power coursing through his veins. He appeared to grow in stature, and his features took on a chiselled, almost granite-like appearance. This was the moment he had been dreaming of. The alchemy, for so many centuries locked away inside the tomb, was finally flowing through him. At last, he would be at one with the gods. He would be truly invincible.

When he reached out his hand in Sienna's direction,

she clutched at her throat in shock. It felt like he had her in a stranglehold. For a few seconds, he watched her writhing and gasping for air. Then he released her from his mental grip and broke into hysterical laughter. Now he could punish his enemies with the power of his mind — surely no one could stand in his way. He would rule both worlds. He would be their god.

But as Sophie watched his madness with increasing horror, the air suddenly chilled, and a veil of mist appeared all around them. It was putrid and stale, and it filled her with an overwhelming sense of foreboding.

Out of that mist, a terrifying shape took form. It was a skeletal figure with torn flesh and the head of an owl. It rose into the air, increasing in size and intensity, and loomed over Silver malevolently. The fire in its eyes glowed like burning coals. Its face was contorted with anger.

As the grotesque figure bore down on him, Sophie noticed a shift in Silver's mood. His eyes widened in confusion, and a twitch developed on the side of his face. It was as if the power had changed and was now turning itself in on him. His breathing became shallow and jerky, and his face was twisted with pain. Desperate to retain his godlike status, he reached out to the apparition imploringly, but to no avail. The figure was consumed with rage and seemed intent on destroying him.

Stumbling around in agony, Silver dropped the Imperium in a state of despair. His eyes were wild and filled with terror. His gait looked unsteady and erratic. Something appeared to be eating away at him from the inside. Where moments earlier, his face had appeared regal and imposing, now he looked haggard and drawn. The power was ebbing away from him. Immortality snatched from his grasp. Collapsing to the ground, he lay there twitching. His sunken eyes were blank and expressionless, as though he had aged a hundred years in just a few seconds.

As the life drained out of Silver's body, the figure turned towards Bunny and the girls. It towered over them menacingly, its fiery gaze intense and terrifying. Sienna and Bunny were rooted to the spot, but Sophie felt a tremendous power surge through her, and without giving it a second thought, she leapt to her feet and rushed towards the shrivelled carcass of Silver.

'No!' Bunny shouted. 'Sophie, don't do it!'

But Sophie had no intention of being stopped. The tiger inside her was now in full flow, her rational mind momentarily sidelined. She picked up the Imperium from where it lay on the ground and flung it with all her force against a nearby tree. With an earsplitting crash, it smashed into a thousand pieces, the flaming fragments lighting up the late evening sky and dancing joyfully like a swarm of rapturous fireflies.

The monstrous figure towered over her, still burning with anger and menace. But as the flaming fragments flickered and died, the image began to fade. It gradually dissipated until its skeletal form was barely perceptible. Almost immediately, the mist cleared and the putrid smell drifted away. Silver's body crumbled and turned to dust, and his ragged remains were taken away on the wind. It was as if he had slowly dissolved.

As the moon broke from behind a cloud, throwing its light down onto the ground, they heard the hoot of an owl and the flapping of wings as something moved away from them into the night. The deathly predator was returning to from where it had come. Sophie didn't move for a moment. She was still trembling with the energy that was surging through her. Then she turned and walked slowly across to where Bunny and Sienna were sitting. She could see at once that a heavy burden had been lifted from Bunny's shoulders. The relics and the Imperium were no more; their accursed threat had gone forever.

'Yum Cimil,' said Bunny, still looking into the space where the monstrous figure had been.

The girls looked at her in confusion.

'Yum Cimil,' she said, 'the Lord of Death. When Silver reunited the Imperium, he connected with the power of the gods and came face to face with Yum Cimil. And what he unleashed was a force that was much more powerful than he could ever be. It destroyed him, just as he intended to destroy us.'

She looked wistfully up into the sky as the last of the mist finally cleared. 'Be careful what you wish for, Mr Silver,' she said, 'lest it should come true.'

Chapter 21

A gust of wind skittered across the garden, picked up the dust that had once been the Imperium, and took it away on its scurrying journey. It was a glorious moment for Bunny. The dread that had stalked her for so many years had finally been swept from her life. A smile lit up her kindly face and, despite the trauma they had just been through, she seemed at peace with the world. Sophie thought she looked ten years younger.

'So the stories about the Imperium weren't just a legend,' said Sienna. 'It really did possess god-like power.'

'Yes,' said Bunny, 'but unfortunately for Mr Silver, it possessed the god-like power of Yum Cimil, the Lord of Death. Those relics must have contained his spirit, to guide whoever was in the tomb through the afterlife, and when Silver completed the puzzle, he unleashed its awesome power.'

'Maybe that's why I felt such a terrible sense of foreboding whenever I was carrying the relic around,' said Sophie.

Bunny nodded in agreement. 'And why I hated having it in the house.'

They sat in silence, thankful that their ordeal was finally over. But their moment of serenity didn't last long. A pair of headlights flashed through the gates, and a large car powered up the driveway towards the house. Before Bunny and the girls had time to react, it was almost in front of them, blinding them with the glare of its lights. Sienna leapt to her feet and prepared herself for battle. If Silver had contacted anyone to help him search the house, they were about to be thrust into another life or death conflict.

As the car skidded to a halt, all four doors flew open and a group of shadowy figures fanned out into the darkness.

'Put your hands up and stay where you are!' someone shouted from behind the dazzling lights.

They heard urgent movement and a woman's voice barking out orders. Seconds later, a tall figure stepped into view. Sophie and Sienna breathed a huge sigh of relief. It was Jutan.

'Thank goodness you're OK,' said Jutan. 'We've been trying to get in touch with you for hours.'

'Silver took our phones,' said Sienna. 'He was waiting for us when we got back to the house.'

Jutan scanned the surrounding area, still on high alert.

'It's OK,' said Sienna. 'He's not here anymore. He found the relics and felt the power of the gods flow through him. Unfortunately for Silver, it was a bigger power than he could handle, and it destroyed him.'

Sophie looked across at Bunny. There was a look of utter confusion on her face.

'It's alright, Bunny,' she said. 'You can put your hands down now. This is Jutan. Sienna and Jutan work together.'

But the introduction didn't make Bunny feel any more comfortable. She looked at the guns Jutan and her agents were carrying and wondered what kind of work this could involve.

'I think we should probably explain to Mrs Robson what's going on here,' said Jutan. 'It seems like you've all been through quite an ordeal.'

They went inside and sat around the large kitchen table while Sophie and Sienna explained what had happened during their eventful day. The trip to Silver's house, the British Museum, and the horror that confronted them on their return to Abbeville House. Jutan listened calmly, without commenting. Sienna's work had clearly impressed her.

'As soon as we received your email, we raided Silver's woodland hideout,' said Jutan. 'Unfortunately, he had already fled from the scene. But when we looked through his papers, we realised he had discovered your true identity. We've been trying to get in touch with you, to pull you out of the operation. We thought it was becoming much too dangerous.'

Bunny was spellbound by the girls' story. She didn't know they had been in so much danger, and the relationship between Sienna and Jutan intrigued her.

'True identity?' she said, with a hint of a smile on her face. 'Is there something you haven't told me about yourself, Sienna?'

Sienna didn't know what to say. She looked at Jutan, hoping to receive some guidance.

'Sienna works for the government on security matters, Mrs Robson,' said Jutan. 'Although I'm hoping you will be kind enough to keep that information between those of us in this room.'

Sophie and Sienna held their breath, wondering how Bunny would react.

'How exciting,' said Bunny, 'and how wonderful for our government to have someone like you on our side, Sienna. Don't worry, Jutan, your secret is safe with me.'

They sat and chatted for a little while longer. Then Jutan thanked Bunny for her hospitality and, before leaving, told Sienna she wouldn't need to report in again until the end of the week.

'I had thought that locating Silver would keep you busy for quite a while,' she said. 'I didn't expect you to wrap this assignment up in just a few days.'

'In that case,' said Sienna, 'would you mind if I stayed on here for a couple of days, Bunny? We've hardly had the chance to get to know one another, and it would be great to catch up with Sophie again.'

'It would be my pleasure,' said Bunny. 'And I'm sure we'll all feel a lot safer knowing a top government agent is staying in the house with us.'

The following morning, Bunny received some good news from the hospital. Albert was feeling much better, and the doctors had decided he was well enough to go home. While Sophie and Sienna did their best to tidy up, Bunny drove to the hospital and ferried Albert back to Abbeville House. There was no problem with the car. It started first time and ran like a dream.

It was a glorious spring afternoon. They sat out in the garden, surrounded by the lovely spring flowers and cherry blossom, and had afternoon tea and a delicious Victoria sponge cake Bunny had bought in the town. It was Albert's favourite. He looked very happy to be home again.

'Thank you so much for keeping Bunny safe while I was in hospital,' he said, reaching out affectionately to Sophie. 'And I'm sorry for dumping you with the responsibility for the relic. But I knew that if it came to the crunch, you would always do the right thing.'

'Did you know you were about to get a visit from Silver?' Sienna asked.

'Well, I knew it was only a matter of time,' said Albert. 'I read about Herbert Hawkins' son being killed during a burglary, and I knew it wouldn't be long before they came for us. That's why I stayed in the museum that night. I was desperate to keep them away from the house.'

'But when they didn't find what they were after, why didn't they come to the house?' said Sophie.

'I told them the relic was in a safe deposit box in central London and gave them an old set of keys and a bogus security code. I hoped it would give us time to disappear for a few days. I didn't think I'd end up unconscious on the floor of a burning building. Luckily for me, there was a superhero staying with us who rushed into the fire and dragged me out. I'll never be able to thank you enough, Sophie. I owe you my life.'

Sophie could feel the emotion welling up inside her. She leaned forward and gave Albert a hug.

'It's great to have you back home again,' she said. 'I'm just sorry that the museum is in such a state.'

'Oh, we can rebuild the museum,' said Bunny, 'but we could never get another Albert.'

'There's one thing I still don't understand,' said Sienna. 'Why didn't you tell us who T.J. Stapleton was?'

Bunny looked a little embarrassed. She shook her head and hesitated for a few seconds before answering.

'Theresa Stapleton,' she said. 'That was my name before I married Albert. Of course, nobody ever called me Theresa. To my parents and siblings I was always Bunny, and that name stayed with me when I became an adult.'

'I still don't understand,' said Sienna.

'I was twenty-one years old when we opened that Mayan tomb. Herbert Hawkins hadn't been keen on taking on a woman as his assistant. He told me the scientific community didn't give much credibility to projects where there was a woman on the dig. But I was well qualified, and my parents had enough money to pay my way. So he agreed to take me, provided I initialised my name to disguise who I really was. From then on, I was T.J. Stapleton. In truth, it wasn't science that had attitudes about women, it was Hawkins. He was a bitter old man who was stuck in the past, and I think he felt threatened by women.'

'So when Albert told me to warn T.J., he was actually talking about you,' said Sophie.

'Did I really say that?' said Albert. 'What a silly old fool I am.'

Bunny reached across and touched his arm.

'Yes, when we first met, Albert always knew me as T.J.,' she said, 'and he still calls me that from time to time. Looking back, I bitterly regret agreeing to change my name, and I wish I could turn back the clock. But it's too late for that.'

'And the address you gave us in Winchester,' said Sophie. 'You knew that was just a wild goose chase, didn't you?'

'I'm afraid so. I wanted to spend the day with Albert, but I couldn't do that and leave you here on your own. It was far too dangerous. And I'm sorry for keeping my voicemail on all day. The hospital said I could sit with Albert, but I had to turn my phone off. I didn't notice the missed calls until I was heading back to the car.'

'That's alright,' said Sophie, smiling warmly. 'We're all OK. That's the main thing.'

A green Land Rover appeared at the far end of the driveway, sailed through the gates, and crunched up the gravel towards them.

'Now, who can this be?' said Albert.

It cruised to a halt in front of the house and, long before he opened the door, Sophie could see that it was being driven by James Adamson. He stepped out onto the path, gave everyone a cheery wave, then opened the rear door to let his dog out. Aslan seemed a lot more bouncy and good-natured than when the girls first met him the previous day. He trotted along at Mr Adamson's side as he strolled across to where they were having tea.

'James,' said Bunny, standing up to greet him, 'how lovely to see you.'

'Hello, Bunny,' said Mr Adamson. 'I hope I'm not intruding. And please don't stand up, Albert. You'll need to preserve your strength to get that museum up and running again.'

They all shook hands vigorously, and Bunny invited Mr Adamson to join them for afternoon tea. While they were talking, Aslan trotted over to where Sophie was sitting. He sat placidly, surveying the gardens, as she stroked his head and ruffled his ears.

'I brought you a contribution to the rebuilt museum,' said Mr Adamson, handing a parcel to Albert. 'And I've spoken to several other members at the Institute. You'll be receiving a lot more contributions in the coming days.'

Albert carefully unwrapped the parcel. When he saw what was inside, his mouth fell open in shock.

'James,' said Bunny, 'you can't give us your Egyptian collection. They're some of the finest specimens in the world.'

'Well, they're only sitting around in a vault at the moment,' said Mr Adamson. 'I'd be much happier if they were available for everyone to see. And where better than the rebuilt museum here at lovely Abbeville House?'

'Thank you, James,' said Albert, looking a little tearful. 'That's incredibly kind of you.'

After they had been talking for a while, Aslan became

a little restless. Sophie noticed it straight away and wondered whether he would like to explore the gardens.

'Mr Adamson,' she said. 'Would you mind if we took Aslan for a walk around the gardens?'

'Not at all,' said Mr Adamson. 'He could probably use a bit of exercise.'

With Aslan trotting along by their side, Sophie and Sienna walked out into the extensive gardens of Abbeville House. He snuffled and sniffed at everything he came across and seemed very comfortable in their company. Sophie picked up a large stick and waved it over her head, causing Aslan to jump up and down with excitement. Then she threw it into the air as far as she could and watched as he charged off after it.

Sienna looked across at her, smiling broadly. She was pleased to see Sophie looking so relaxed. After a lifelong fear of dogs, she had finally found a canine friend she felt comfortable with.

'Wow, look at you,' said Sienna, 'messing around with a big dog. You'll be wrestling bears next.'

'Oh yeah,' said Sophie, smiling back at her. 'Bears, sharks, alligators, I'll take them all on. I'm still not picking up a spider, though. You have to draw the line somewhere.'

Also by A.B. Martin
Kestrel Island

In a sleepy English seaside town, Sophie Watson is enjoying a peaceful holiday in the sunshine. But when she befriends a mysterious and charismatic girl called Sienna, she is drawn into a heart-stopping adventure where the future security of the world may be under threat.

To find out the truth, they must go to Kestrel Island. The plot they uncover is more mind-blowing than they could have possibly imagined.

Sophie's life is about to change forever.

If you enjoyed this book…

Thank you so much for checking out Sophie and Sienna's latest adventure.

If you enjoyed reading the book, I'd be very grateful if you could spend a minute leaving a review on the book's Amazon page. Even one short sentence would be very much appreciated.

Reviews make a real difference to authors. They help other readers get a feel for the book, and I'd also be very interested to hear your thoughts on the story.

Many thanks for your help.

Acknowledgements

Many thanks to Dane at ebooklaunch.com for the wonderful cover design. And special thanks to my wife, Annie Burchell. Her detailed scrutiny of the manuscript and inspirational thoughts and ideas played a major part in the development of this story.

About the author

A.B. Martin is an English author who writes thrilling middle-grade adventure stories and intriguing mysteries.

Before becoming an author, he wrote extensively for television and radio and performed comedy in a vast array of venues, including the world-famous London Palladium.

Silver's Gold is the fourth book in the Sophie Watson series. It was published in May 2021.

He lives in London, England, with his wife and daughter.

Printed in Great Britain
by Amazon